THE HODGKISS MYSTERIES

Hodgkiss and the Eruv
Hodgkiss and the Empty Room
Hodgkiss and the Ten Dollar Note

PETER SINCLAIR

About the author

Peter Sinclair has spent most of his working life writing. He began reporting courts and councils in rural Orange (NSW) in the late 1950s then worked briefly for The Sydney Daily Telegraph where, because of his fluent shorthand, he was sentenced first to  report local councils then banished to the Coroner's Court.

He'd had enough of sudden death and murder when opportunity knocked and he joined the staff of a new, large weekly paper in Sydney's northern suburbs, The North Shore Times where he was soon reporting councils again.

In 1965, he climbed over the journalistic fence to work as press secretary for a succession of NSW cabinet ministers (both Liberal and Labor) until 1991. Since then, he has made guest reappearances to help out in the PR sections of government departments.

His absorbing hobby is playing the piano. He has made a number of CDs in very limited editions. The titles tell it all: Peter Murders Mozart, Wrecks Rachmaninoff and Desecrates Debussy. He says he gives them away to people he doesn't like!

He has been married to Margaret for fifty-seven years and they have two sons; Sam, who is married to Carolyn with one son, Harry, 18, and Patrick who is married to Beejai with twin boys, Jackson and Zachary, aged 13.

Published in Australia by Peter Sinclair
First published in Australia 2020
Copyright © Peter Sinclair 2020
Cover design, typesetting: WorkingType Studio

The right of Peter Sinclair to be identified as the Author of the Work has been asserted in accordance with the Copyright, Designs and Patents Act 1988.

The Hodgkiss Mysteries Volume XVI
ISBN: 978-0-6450020-8-9
Sinclair, Peter
pp222

For Margaret

Author's Note

I t has been no easy task to assemble material in order to reconstruct these accounts of the extraordinary contributions which Edgar Hodgkiss made to criminal detection over the years in which he was active in the field.

Hodgkiss himself kept no records.

When he suggested solutions to investigations being undertaken by his son-in-law, Detective Sergeant Donald Burke, Hodgkiss was convinced that he was merely stating the obvious and that his contributions were unremarkable and not worthy of record.

However, this presumption that he was 'merely stating the obvious' was frequently the cause of acrimony between himself and Sergeant Burke who resented the implied slur on his own powers of observation.

Fortunately for readers of these reports (and for posterity), Hodgkiss's daughter, Esme, kept detailed records in a series of exercise books which she has kindly made available to those of us interested in researching and recording the contributions made by this unique character.

Jan Campbell-Jones, the General Manager of Kanundda Council during this testing period of its history, also kindly consented to assist by releasing relevant documents from her personal files and from council's own official records system.

Ms Campbell-Jones also graciously agreed to be interviewed and has given accounts of many of these extraordinary events from her point of view, relying on her remarkable powers of recall to provide in some cases verbatim accounts of significant conversations. In addition she has allowed us access to the many emails that passed between Hodgkiss and herself. Hodgkiss, of course, had deleted these emails from his laptop within days, or in some instances, within hours of transmission.

I am indebted also to the many members of community organisations who supported Edgar Hodgkiss in his various campaigns against what he saw as the deficiencies of Kanundda Council and who have helped me verify many important details.

Readers of these records should note that they do not appear in chronological order therefore minor temporal inconsistencies may appear.

Many incidents in which Hodgkiss played an important role have not yet been committed to paper and many others, unfortunately, will never appear on the public record.

On occasions both the innocent and the guilty must be protected.

Peter Sinclair,

Lillimoor, 2011

Hodgkiss and the Eruv

Esme Burke looked up from the newspaper spread open before her on the round redwood table on the back deck of the Burke's Lillimoor home.

'Dad, what on earth is an eruv?' she asked.

'An eruv? What makes you ask about that?' demanded her father, Edgar Hodgkiss, who was slumped uncomfortably in a director's chair at the other end of the deck, puzzling over the chess problem which he had clipped neatly from one of the weekend papers.

Esme held up a page of the local newspaper, the *Northern Star.* 'Look here, Dad. There's a whole column of letters to the editor about it in the *Star.* They want to build one of these eruvs at St James and some of the locals are protesting about it. Don't you know what it is … an eruv?'

Hodgkiss frowned. 'I'm not sure, but I think it has something to do with how Jewish people observe their Sabbath. If I remember correctly an eruv is an artificial boundary line that enables people of the Jewish faith who live inside it to move about on their Sabbath without observing all of the rather odd archaic restrictions that normally apply; carrying items around, pushing prams or things like wheelchairs, using walking frames or even pressing the button to change traffic lights.'

Esme shook her head. 'But that's crazy. Why shouldn't people be allowed to do normal every-day things like that?'

Hodgkiss shrugged. 'Well, crazy or not, those are some of the rules their religion sets down, like it or not.'

He turned his attention once more to the chess problem, white to play and mate in three moves. Hodgkiss had reached a provisional solution that involved white making a waiting move with his king, and he was now testing his solution for flaws.

A few minutes later Esme looked up again. 'It says here that if they're going to make this eruv it means they'll have to put up a whole lot of poles and wires. I can understand why some people might object to that.'

But Hodgkiss was too absorbed in the chess problem even to offer a comment.

Esme continued. 'Some of these letter-writers are getting pretty hot under the collar. Listen to this one, Dad.'

Hodgkiss turned and held up a hand. 'Esme. If I was the least bit interested in the subject of eruvs I would read the letters for myself. As it is I have no desire to ...'

Esme cut him off. 'All right. So you don't want to know about it. But there's no need to be so rude.' She put down the paper, pushed back the curved bench and headed for the sliding aluminium door to the family room.

'What do you want for your lunch, Dad?' she asked. 'The usual, I suppose.'

Hodgkiss grunted agreement without looking up.

But when Esme returned ten minutes later with two cheese and tomato sandwiches cut in halves with their crusts cut off and set out symmetrically on a large plastic plate, her father had taken her place at the redwood table, the newspaper open before him.

'I detect a most unpleasant note of anti-Semitism in some of these letters,' he said. Without lifting his eyes from the page Hodgkiss took the plate from his daughter and set it down on the table beside the newspaper. 'In fact, I am almost moved to take some of these nasty bigots to task for their irrational and intolerant views.'

'Really! Well that's a bit of a surprise, Dad, because five minutes ago when I wanted to read out one of those letters you didn't want to hear it, now all of a sudden ...'

'Esme, you know as well as I that I have always taken an active interest in civic affairs so why ever you should think that ...'

'Yes, and quite a few people around here would say you take rather too much interest'

'Yes, I dare say you're right,' said Hodgkiss, smiling grimly and biting into a sandwich. 'And they would be our so-called civic leaders on Kanundda Council and their cronies who are more interested in feathering their own nests than advancing the good of the community.'

Esme shook her head. 'Dad. Sometimes you are just so incredibly ... full of yourself.'

'Full of myself!!! Is that how you characterize my efforts to ...'

'Oh, for heavens' sake Dad, don't get on your high horse. You know that I've always supported what you've done in the past to try to keep the council honest ... well, nearly always.'

'And what are you two squabbling about?' Detective Sergeant Donald Burke stepped out onto the deck from the family room, a mug of tea in one hand.

'We were not squabbling,' said Hodgkiss stiffly. 'Esme and I were discussing the plans for the eruv at St James.'

Donald's eyebrows rose. 'Don't talk to me about the ruddy eruv.'

'Why's that, Donald?' Esme asked. 'I'm surprised you've even heard of it.'

'Yeah, well, I've heard more about it than I care to. I can tell you that there's a lot of unpleasantness brewing about that business.'

'Unpleasantness ... involving the police?' Hodgkiss asked. 'What sort of unpleasantness? Threats? Physical violence?'

'No violence ... not yet anyway. But plenty of threats. All anonymous of course'

'And you're taking them seriously?'

Donald shrugged. 'We have to. There're some pretty influential people involved.'

'Like whom?'

'Dad, this is confidential police business. I can't go into details.' He sat down opposite Hodgkiss and blew across the top of his steaming mug then took a cautious sip.

Hodgkiss continued. 'I suppose it's all nasty racist anti-Semitic invective.'

Donald nodded. 'Yeah. There's plenty of that sort of stuff. Typed notes with swastikas drawn on them making silly threats. I'd have thought that people around here were above that sort of thing.'

'Of course there's a lot of *them* living at St James, isn't there?' said Esme.

'*Them*. What do you mean by *them*?' Hodgkiss demanded angrily. 'I thought your mother and I had brought you up with a little more tolerance for your fellow man.'

'I wasn't being intolerant, Dad,' Esme protested.

'Well, it certainly sounded like it to me ... referring to Jewish people as *them.*'

'Yes, but Esme's right, isn't she, Dad?' said Donald. 'And of course that's part of the problem. They all congregate in the one area. In a kind of enclave. But as soon as they run into a problem they want the rest of the community to chip in and bail them out.'

'Exactly what are you saying, Donald?' Hodgkiss demanded, unable to suppress a quiver of anger in his voice. 'Do you object when a minority group looks to the rest of the community for a helping hand to make their lives a little less arduous?'

Donald looked slightly abashed. 'No, of course not. But in this case I reckon they've made the problems for themselves with all those silly rules about not being able to even push a pram or carry a bunch of keys in their pockets.'

'It may seem silly to you, Donald, but this is the way these people have lived their lives for thousands of years ...'

'Then why change now? Why ask to build this eruv thing so they can get around their silly old rules?'

'I would say there's a perfectly sensible explanation,' said Hodgkiss, 'that is, if you stop to think about if for more than two minutes at a time. All those old religious rules were laid down thousands of years ago. They just don't apply any more to modern-day living. Don't forget, once you couldn't drive a car without a man walking in front carrying a flag. I doubt if there were many traffic lights around in the time of Moses. This is simply a sensible way of adapting their religion to contemporary living. Do you really object to that?'

'Well, I don't personally,' said Donald, chastened now. 'But there are plenty of people around the St James area who do.'

'Yes. I know that,' said Hodgkiss holding up a page of the

Star. 'And I think it's a disgrace. Particularly since more than one of the people who have put their names to these letters never miss a chance to present themselves as part of our educated elite. Damned ignorant, intolerant bigots. That's all they are.'

'That's all very well, Dad,' said Esme, 'but all these posts and wires that have to be put up to make this imaginary boundary of theirs; they're going to cost money, right? I don't see why the rest of us should pay to make their lives easier.'

'You needn't worry your head about that, my girl. It won't cost you a penny. If it ever happens, that is. The Jewish community will bear the cost of setting it up, or that's what it says in this letter.' Hodgkiss pointed to one of columns in the *Star's* double page spread of letters to the editor. 'This one here; the one signed by M Carpenter. He says the Jewish community at St James will bear all the costs of installing it.'

'Carpenter, eh?' said Donald. 'That doesn't sound very Jewish.'

Esme shrugged. 'Well, as long as it doesn't cost the rest of us anything, I suppose it's all right then,'

Hodgkiss moved into didactic mode. 'Really, Esme, I am seriously disappointed at your attitude to this matter. I would have thought that one of the tests of the quality of any civilized community was the way in which it treats minorities. You seem to begrudge the Jews in St James even this minor concession.'

'But Dad, it could have been quite expensive and it wouldn't have been fair if all the people who didn't want it had to pay to put it up. After all, it's not going to do anything for the rest of the people who live there.'

'Well, it's not going to cost you anything, my girl, so relax,' said Hodgkiss. 'It says in this letter from M Carpenter that nearly all of the wires that have to be put up to enclose their area will be strung between existing telegraph poles. Just a few will have to be attached to new poles erected on private land and he says that the organisers already have approval from the private land owners in all these cases. So I can't see any reason why it shouldn't go ahead unless of course the bigots who object, obviously for purely racial reasons, can persuade our gutless council to vote the project down.'

'Do you mean it still has to be approved by council?'

'Of course. At the moment the whole thing is only at the stage of a development application. I've no doubt that as we speak the intolerant anti-Semites who are opposed to it will be working on individual councillors to vote against it'

Donald asked: 'So you think it's possible that the whole thing still might never go ahead?'

'I'd say that's highly likely, particularly in view of your news that a minority of nasty racists is already busily issuing threats. But even if council is intimidated into rejecting the project an appeal to the Land and Environment Court would probably succeed, particularly in view of the fact that eruvs already exist in many cities around the world; obviously in more enlightened communities than that lot of bigots who seem to think they rule the roost at St James.'

Hodgkiss's commentary was interrupted by the sound of the cordless phone in the hall ringing.

Esme said: 'You get it, Donald. It'll probably be for you anyway.'

But Esme was mistaken. When Donald returned clutching the handset he set it down on the table in front of his father-in-law. 'It's for you, Dad. It's your friend at the council.'

At once Esme came to her feet and headed hurriedly for the sliding door. 'Then I'll leave you to get on with it,' she announced tartly, pulling the door closed behind her with a thud.

Hodgkiss picked up the handset and put a hand over the mouth piece. 'Really, Donald, Esme will have to learn not to behave in this childish fashion.'

Donald shrugged. 'You don't have to persuade me, Dad, but she'll take a bit of convincing.'

The reason for Esme's indignant departure in the direction of the kitchen was the identity of the caller, described by Donald as 'your friend at the council.' This was a reference to the General Manager of Kanundda Council, Jan Campbell-Jones. Esme, who had heard accounts of Jan's sexual exploits, was extremely uneasy at any contacts between the attractive general manager and her father.

'Yes, Jan. And what is the purpose of your call this fine morning?' Hodgkiss asked. 'No fresh disaster looming on the local government horizon, I trust.'

In her spacious office at the front of the Kanundda Council Chambers building on the Northern Highway at nearby Grattan, Jan set down a Styrofoam cup of black coffee on a cork coaster. 'No, Hodgkiss, or nothing more disastrous than usual. I was only calling to let you know that last night I left in your letter box an envelope that may be of interest. No doubt you remember mentioning to me that you were planning to write a history of unsolved crime in Kanundda.'

'Yes, of course.'

'And how is that magnum opus progressing?'

'It is progressing slowly. Unfortunately I have been sidetracked on a number of occasions by the activities of contemporary criminals whose activities have required Donald's attention and thus my assistance.'

'Hodgkiss, I know the feeling. Getting sidetracked is part

of everyday life in this administration. It is impossible to work solidly on anything without trivial interruptions. However, yesterday it fell to my lot to attend a meeting of the Kanundda Historical Society and while talking to one of the members after all the official business was over and done with, this person, a lady, related a morsel of crime from the distant past of our suburbs which may well be of interest to you in your researches.'

'Really, and what was the nature of this unsolved crime?'

'It was a missing persons matter. Two people disappeared, two migrants from the continent shortly before the war.'

'And which war would this have been. There has been quite a number of wars in my lifetime.'

'World War Two. The missing persons — there were two of them, two brothers — had recently arrived from the continent — heaven knows where exactly — and apparently had settled somewhere in Kanundda. Where, exactly, I could not say. Donald may be able to find something about them from the police department's old records if they were reported missing.'

Hodgkiss shook his head. 'Knowing the efficiency of our police service I doubt that very much. But I suppose I could give it a try. These brothers; do you know their name?'

'Yes, the way it was told to me it sounded like Klempner. But I couldn't be sure of the spelling.'

'And the person who told you about these missing persons; who was that?'

'She's a long term resident of Kanundda. She's already written a history of the municipality and is doing further research now for a second edition to up date the original. I have already emailed her particulars to you.'

'Well thank you very much for your consideration, Jan.

It is much appreciated. I regret that my work on the manuscript has lapsed rather seriously due to diversions provided by Donald's investigations, but this should provide the impetus I need to overcome my inertia.

When Hodgkiss had disconnected the call, Donald inquired: 'And what was that about?'

Hodgkiss put down the handset on the open pages of the *Star*. 'You may recall that some time ago I announced the intention to prepare a monograph on unsolved crime in Kanundda's early days. Jan Campbell-Jones has thoughtfully provided me with a contact who may be in a position to provide me with details of one such crime.'

'And what sort of crime is it?'

'A missing persons case, I understand.'

Donald protested. 'But missing persons cases aren't necessarily crimes, you know, Dad. Sometimes they disappear and stay disappeared and no one ever knows why or where, and other times they just turn up. Often there's no crime involved.'

'I realise that, Donald,' Hodgkiss said with a display of impatience. 'But since Jan was thoughtful enough to bring the matter to my attention I shall at least take the trouble to follow it up. In the meantime perhaps you might test the capacity of your official sources to see what became of the case. It involves two brothers by the unusual name of Klempner, last known address somewhere in Kanundda.'

'I'll need a bit more than that to go on. When are they supposed to have gone missing?'

'Some time before the second world war. That's all I know.'

Donald nodded. 'OK. I'll get the boys to run a check, but since it happened that far back someone probably would have to do a manual search through the old records, if they're even

still in the building, that is. And it won't be easy to find someone with the spare time for that sort of thing. Present day
crime keeps us plenty busy without bothering about crime
from the distant past.'

'I understand that Donald, but I'd appreciate anything you
can turn up,' said Hodgkiss. He picked up the last triangle of
sandwich and bit into it.

*   *   *

Hodgkiss had never been in such a room in all his life; never
in all his sixty-nine years. Why, there wasn't even a window.
No. That couldn't be right. Probably there was a window hidden behind that ancient tapestry hanging on the far wall, so
faded now that the pattern was indecipherable.

Then there was all those ornaments and the furnish-
ings; the ancient dark bureau that took up half the room and
other smaller pieces, tables, what-nots, all littered with ornaments of china and art glass, all things from an earlier age,
or century.

Hodgkiss was no slouch when it came to recognising a
valuable antique when he saw it and most of these things
seemed to his eye to be authentic and valuable. The small
figurines were early, probably Meissen, as were some of the
cups and saucers in the china cabinet wedged tight between
the desk and a sofa table behind the two-seater lounge.

Then there was the old lady whom Jan had mentioned,
sitting opposite him; sharp eyed, attentive. She could have
been the model for one or more of those little porcelain figures with their quaint old-fashioned clothes in faded pastel
colours.

Mrs Judge was the secretary/treasurer of the Kanundda

Historical Society. The jumble of papers strewn over the antique desk and jumbled in untidy heaps on a grandmother chair and on the Turkey rug that covered much of the floor, testified to her relentless activity.

'Yes, I remember about those two, the fellows who disappeared, the Klempners. People around here are not likely to forget those two beauties.' Her accent was thick, continental.

'Really. Why is that?' Hodgkiss asked.

Mrs Judge wrinkled her nose. 'Nasty, nasty people.'

'Nasty in what way.'

'Every way, Mr Hodgkiss. Every way you could possibly think of. They were greedy. They could never have enough money. And violent.'

'When did you meet them, Mrs Judge, and where?'

'I never met them, not personally. But I heard all about them through others. People whom I had known for a long time ... people whose word and judgment I trusted. Unfortunately most of these people now are enjoying the company of the great majority of mankind.'

'And these are people who knew the Klempners.'

Mrs Judge nodded grimly. 'Oh, yes. They knew the Klempner boys very well indeed.'

'Did they know them here, in Australia, or overseas? Klempner does not sound like a traditional English name, does it?'

Mrs Judge smiled. 'How can one tell what is a truly English name. Judge sounds frightfully, frightfully British does it not? The sort of name that might well belong to a genuine blue-blooded English gentleman.'

Hodgkiss nodded. 'I'd wondered about that.'

'When my late husband and I came to Australia in the thirties our name was Richter. In German Richter means judge.' She chuckled pleasantly. 'You see, Mr Hodgkiss, in those days it was not quite the thing to have a name that sounded even faintly Germanic. It could work to your disadvantage.'

'No doubt,' Hodgkiss agreed.

'And Klempner, for your information, is the German word for plumber. Although the Klempner boys were not plumbers it would be true to say they were not at all averse to getting their hands dirty.'

'But, unlike you, they did not actually change their names.

'No. They may have meant to do so but they never did it, so far as I know.'

'And these friends of yours who told you what they knew about the Klempners, did they meet them in Australia or before they arrived here. I assume they, too, came here from Germany.'

'Both. They knew the Klempners in Germany before Hitler took over and then here, too.'

'When you say "here" do you mean here in Australia or that they lived locally … here in Kanundda somewhere?'

'Oh, locally. The Klempners definitely lived locally. I couldn't say for sure if they ever lived here in St James, but they were certainly known here. There was an incident involving them.'

'Incident. What kind of incident was that?'

'There was a crime committed and it was the Klempners that were responsible.'

'A crime. What? A violent crime?'

'It was something that happened at the hotel where they were staying at Kylerbrin. On the main road.'

'That may have been the Travellers Inn. It's been there for well over a hundred years. What kind of an incident was it?

'The story is that they took some money from the owner. They said that he owed them money and they beat him to make him open the safe.'

'Then what happened? Were the police called?'

'No. Nothing happened. There were no police. The publican was too frightened. Perhaps he really owed them the money. Who knows? People said the Klempners were involved in all sorts of dealings; lending money and making people pay for different things.'

'For protection, you think?'

'Yes, protection money. It could be.'

'And what did people think had happened when they disappeared?'

Mrs Judge shrugged elaborately. 'Everybody was so pleased. They hoped that they would never return … and they didn't.'

'And were there any theories about what had happened to them. Someone must have had some ideas about it.'

'Oh yes. Everyone had some idea about what had happened, but of course no one could be sure, could they? No one really knew. They just disappeared. Both of them.' She waved a hand. 'And good riddance.'

Hodgkiss nodded. 'And these other people who knew the Klempners … friends of yours; do any of them still live around here. I'd like to talk to them too.'

Mrs Judge shook her head. 'No. They're all gone. All except old Oscar Carpenter. He lives now in one of those old people's homes and he's completely gaga now, or so they say. I think his son still lives somewhere around here though.'

Hodgkiss rose. He was about to make his farewells when a thought struck him. 'What do you think about this idea for an eruv? I suppose you've heard about that.'

Mrs Judge smiled. 'That's young people for you. Anything for an easy life.'

You don't approve then?' Hodgkiss asked.

She shrugged elaborately. 'I don't approve. I don't disapprove. Who am I to tell young people how they should live their lives these days? Putting up an eruv will make life a little easier for the young people and God knows they have enough problems these days without having to observe all the old laws. Good luck to them I say. I hope it happens. It's happened already in lots of other cities around the world. Why not here?'

'An eminently sensible attitude, I would say, Mrs Judge. May I congratulate you.'

She smiled. 'You may, Mr Hodgkiss.'

'But not everyone in the local community shares your attitude, do they?'

'No. But we Jews are accustomed to that kind of thing. Maybe one day ...'

She left the rest of the thought unspoken.

*   *   *

'Thank you, Jan. I had a very interesting discussion with Mrs Judge.'

Hodgkiss was sitting on the end of his bed in the front room of the Burke's home, the handset from the cordless phone pressed to an ear.

Jan had been sitting, reading, in her official staff sedan, parked under a huge gum tree beside Spring Vale Road in St James, when the tiny blue mobile phone in her handbag had played its ring tone, a tinny rendition of *The Ride of the Valkyries*.

Jan smiled. 'And what about Donald? Has he turned up anything? Frankly I'm astounded that he showed any willingness to become involved in this little project of yours.'

'I certainly would not have used the word "willingness" to describe his attitude. Anyway, he's convinced my request will prove to be a lost cause since any records, if they ever existed, of a missing persons report about the Klempner brothers made more than eighty years ago are not likely to be readily retrieved; at least not without considerable effort and expenditure of what he described as valuable police resources.'

'Well, I must admit he has a point, Hodgkiss. I'd be astonished if they have records of missing persons going back that far. I know council's records from that period are by no means complete.'

'No doubt. Nevertheless I would be obliged if he makes the effort, or at least delegates some constable to the task. I doubt if he could spare any time from his latest vital assignment which is, I understand, assessing the results of the activities of Neighbourhood Watch groups.'

'Now, don't you belittle the efforts of Neighbourhood Watch, Hodgkiss. It is a valuable scheme. And ...'

'Yes, yes, I know all about that,' said Hodgkiss peevishly. 'Donald frequently reminds me of how effective it is. Yet crime remains rampant in our suburbs.'

'Perhaps,' Jan conceded. 'And what exactly did old Mrs Judge tell you last night?'

'Well, for one thing she told me that her name, when she came to Australia in the thirties, was Richter which, she assured me, translates into Judge in English. She also mentioned that Klempner is German for plumber although the Klempner brothers, so far as she knows, had not made any move to change their names when they disappeared.'

Jan nodded. 'Yes, there was a lot of name changing among the migrant families that arrived here around those years; pre- and post-war. For obvious reasons. And what else did she tell you?'

'Very little actually. Just that they were unfavourably known in the St James area; they were involved in some sort of violent incident probably involving the landlord of the Travellers Inn and were suspected of being standover men.'

'And that's it?'

'So far. But my inquiries have scarcely begun. I thought I might have a talk to one Oscar Carpenter who lives in a retirement village somewhere locally. Mrs Judge said that he might have some information about the notorious vanishing Klempner brothers. I'll have to try to track him down.'

'Well, good luck there, Hodgkiss.' She hesitated. 'Wasn't one of the letters to the editor in the Star this week about the eruv signed by someone by the name of Carpenter? I think it was.'

Hodgkiss nodded. 'Yes. I believe you're right. M Carpenter I think the letter was signed. He may be able to tell me where to find old Oscar. I might try to track him down through the phone book and give him a call. I suppose it's possible they're related. Now before I go; is there anything new in your vast administration that I should know about?'

'"That you should know about," Jan repeated for emphasis. 'Heaven alone knows what you *think* you should know about. However, I have a sneaking suspicion that most of the councillors would have another view on the matter. As far as they're concerned you already find out far too much for their comfort as your letters to the editor have shown frequently in the past.'

'Never mind about that,' said Hodgkiss impatiently. 'You

know what I mean. Are they up to anything that I should know about; for example, what new scam are they trying to hide that I should be in a position to bring to public notice? Are you about to proclaim any new areas under your so-called children's playgrounds programme?'

Jan was amazed. 'Now, how on earth did you know about that, Edgar?'

'It was the proverbial little bird that mentioned it to me. My informant advised that council is about to proclaim, without any public announcement of course, a number of new areas in which the fortunate gentleman who acts as council's estate agent in these matters, may buy up properties with a view to on-selling them to council for re-zoning. The story for public consumption has been that these properties are to be converted into children's playgrounds. But experience has shown that what usually happens with this land is that council on-sells it to a developer friend of the mayor and his faction then, after a discreet time has elapsed, the land is re-zoned for high rise and the lucky developer makes a killing. Then the mayor and his cronies receive lavish kick-backs from the grateful developer.'

Jan shook her head. 'Goodness, Hodgkiss, what an imagination you have.'

'There's no imagination involved unfortunately, you know that as well as I.'

'These claims are easy to make, Hodgkiss, but the very devil to make stick.

'I can't see why. You know which properties council has brought from this favoured operator. You know how much council paid for them and what became of them later.'

'You appear to assume, Hodgkiss, that I have open entrée to everything that happens in this place. Nothing could be further from the truth. The mayor and his cronies have two senior staff in their pockets and without their cooperation I am completely frozen out of the tight little circle where all these shabby deals are done. The transactions are all declared Commercial In Confidence. The Senior Planning officer acts as council's liaison with the estate agent and he, as you probably are aware, is the mayor's cousin. It's all tied up tighter than a bass drum.'

Hodgkiss tut-tutted. 'Then can you at least tell me where these new areas are located? I would have thought that there was already ample opportunity for the mayor's crony in the real estate business to rip off unsuspecting property owners in the existing proclaimed areas without offering him even bigger ponds in which to do his fishing for the unsuspecting.'

'Apparently not. I suppose there's no harm in telling you , because only last week I authorized the planning staff to post out letters to residents in the new areas affected, so no doubt the mayor's friend will be running around as we speak, making offers to homeowners in these new areas.'

'And where are these new areas mostly to be found?'

'They're concentrated in St James. The mayor thinks that land there is cheap relative to the rest of Kanundda, consequently when council acquires the land from the mayor's agent it will be less expensive than properties acquired elsewhere.'

'No doubt. But haven't council's accountants yet woken up to the fact that there is a scam going on here; that the agent buys the land for a certain undisclosed figure then on-sells it to council at a huge profit. He must realise that council could have approached the homeowners directly and cut out the profiteering middle-man.'

'Hodgkiss, there is no likelihood of any change being

made to this programme so long as the mayor distributes the kick-back from the developer — often tens of thousands of dollars — among his cronies. After all, he's got to keep them happy if he wishes to hold on to his majority on council. And as for the accountants; the head partner of the firm that does council's books is Cr Gregory's cousin, and Gregory, in case you don't already know it, is the leader of the mayor's little cabal of sycophantic supporters.'

Hodgkiss shook his head angrily. 'That is a truly disgraceful state of affairs. And you do nothing to circumvent it.'

'Steady on there, Hodgkiss. I have done all I can within the limited scope available to me. I am at risk of dismissal if I disclose anything that takes place in any committee of council and it is always in one or other of the committees that all of this chicanery take place. Details of the purchases from the agents never see the light of day. Nor do the prices the agents paid for the properties or the prices council paid the agent; not the names of the previous owners of the properties, not the date of purchase, not even the size of the land on which the houses stand. All of this is declared commercial in confidence — those magic words that enable council to keep the scam going.'

'Still, surely some way can be found to bring this scam to an end.'

'If you think of something, Hodgkiss, may I be the first to hear of it.' She leaned forward and twisted the key in the ignition. The motor barked into life. 'Meanwhile, there are some of us who must earn a living. Good luck with your criminology research.'

Hodgkiss cut the connection, rose from the end of the bed and walked out to the hall where he took a telephone directory from the single narrow drawer in the telephone table. He rifled through the pages to the Cs then searched for an M Carpenter in St James. He took a pencil from a small leather cup kept beside the phone and noted a phone number on a slip of paper taken from his wallet. He put back the directory then returned with the handset to his bedroom. He settled again on the end of the bed and dialed.

'Good morning,' he said when the call was answered. 'Is that Mr Carpenter. Mr M Carpenter.'

'Yes, this is Michael Carpenter. Who is that?'

'My name is Hodgkiss, Edgar Hodgkiss. I am anxious to contact a Mr Oscar Carpenter, an elderly gentleman whom I believe is at present residing in a nursing home in this area. Do you know him?'

'Oscar Carpenter is my father.'

'Good. I'd hoped that might be the case. I would like to speak to him in connection with some research I am doing. A lady from the local historical society, a Mrs Judge, said your father may be able to assist me.'

'Research. What kind of research are you doing, Mr Hodgkiss?' Carpenter asked, guardedly.

'It concerns the disappearance more than fifty years ago of two people, brothers, by the name of Klempner. Have you heard that name before?'

The response came too quickly. 'No. Sorry to disappoint you.'

'Very well. Now if you would be so good as to give me your father's address I'll ring and make an arrangement to drop in and see if he knows anything that might be of assistance. By the way, was it you who wrote the letter about the eruv in the latest issue of the *Star*?'

'Yes, that was me. Why? Are you for or against?'

'I'm for. Very much for. I have nothing but contempt for

the miserable racists who are trying to stand in the way. There is no possible reason for opposition other than anti-Semitism.'

'Spot on, Mr Hodgkiss.'

'I noticed when I wrote down your number from the phone book that the street where you live appears to be on the very edge of the eruv area.'

'Yes, that's so. In fact we'll have to let them put up a pole in our front yard to make the final connection. There are no telegraph poles on our side of the street to string up the wire so it'll have to be connected in our front yard.'

'And I've no doubt your father is in favour of the eruv too.'

Carpenter chuckled. 'Interesting you should ask. Dad was very much in favour of it until I told him about the pole in our front yard. Then all of a sudden he wouldn't hear another word about it.'

'But the few poles that have to go up on private property to make the final connections — they won't be very intrusive, will they?'

'No, of course not. You'll hardly notice them. But then you know the way old people get … don't like change.'

'I do indeed,' said Hodgkiss. 'I suppose your home has been in the family quite a while, has it?'

'I'm the third generation to live in this house. But unfortunately I'll be the last.'

'Oh, and why is that, if I may ask?'

'We've been re-zoned into one of those areas which council has set aside for children's playgrounds. I had an estate agent beating on the door yesterday asking to buy me out. The offer was just too good to refuse. It's for the council, you know. The fellow is trying to buy up all the houses on our side of the road.'

'Is he indeed. I must say I've always admired the houses on your block. They look like real quality.'

Carpenter nodded. 'Yes. They're all very well built. The same fellow put them all up before the war …five of them in a row. Dad's sometimes thought about getting together with some of the neighbours to have them heritage listed so that future generations can't touch them.'

'And what does you father think of your decision to sell the house? He might not be too pleased.'

Carpenter lowered his eyes. 'He doesn't know yet. I haven't screwed up the courage to tell him. I know he'll hit the roof. He thought even digging up his precious lawn to put in a little pole to make the connection for the eruv was the end of the world. Imagine what he'll say about selling the house and having it knocked down for a playground. I hate to even think of it, but I'll have to tell him.'

'But he couldn't stop the deal going through, I suppose.'

Carpenter hesitated. 'No. He lets me handle all his business affairs these days. Not that there's all that much business to handle.'

'Well, I hope this plan for a playground doesn't cause your father too much trauma. Now, if you would be so good as to give me his address I might drop in to see him at the nursing home some time tomorrow'

*   *   *

The Rosemount was in a quite backstreet of East Kylerbrin. Seen from the front it appeared little different from the other comfortable Federation bungalows that lined the street. But as Hodgkiss approached the entry, which had been relocated from the front veranda to the side of the building, he saw that the house had been massively extended. Three stories, built onto the rear in harmonious brick, stepped down the sloping land to the national park which adjoined the back boundary.

Inside the building the pleasing effect of the high ceilings, ornate plaster cornices and richly moulded skirting boards was overwhelmed by the smell of disinfectant and other odours that Hodgkiss had come to associate with old age, illness and incontinence.

He approached a nurse's station at one side of the entry hall. 'I've come to visit Mr Oscar Carpenter,' he announced to the young woman dressed smartly in a blue and white nurses' uniform who was seated at a desk, a student's lamp focused down onto the pages of a medical text book.

The young nurse looked up and smiled. 'Goodness,' she said. 'Mr Carpenter *is* popular today. He already has someone with him. I suppose he won't object to one more.'

She inserted a bookmark in the page, closed her book, turned off the lamp and rose. 'Would you like to follow me.'

Hodgkiss followed the nurse along a dim, echoing corridor with doors closed on either side.

'How many … er, patients do you have here?' he asked.

'We're not a big place,' the nurse replied. 'About twenty five is our limit. We're full up at the moment. Why? Were you thinking of …'

'Oh, no,' said Hodgkiss quickly with an emphatic shake of his head.

'This is Mr Carpenter's room,' said the nurse applying her knuckles briskly to a door with a number seven painted amateurishly in black on the beige surface. Inside the room, voices raised in argument in some foreign language which Hodgkiss suspected was German, fell suddenly silent.

Then the door was pulled open and a short man, stout

with silver hair, stood in the doorway. 'Yes, nurse. What is it?'
He was obviously not pleased at the interruption.

'Another visitor for Mr Carpenter,' the nurse announced
pleasantly.

The man seemed about to protest when a voice from
within the room called: 'Who is it, Henry?'

'I don't know. It's someone. Some stranger.'

The voice continued; 'No one coming to see me can be
any stranger than you. Bring him in.'

With a grunt of annoyance the short man stood to one
side and Hodgkiss entered the room.

Against the right hand wall was a standard hospital bed
made of iron rails and posts and in the bed, propped up on
a mass of pillows, was an old man with a dense black beard
streaked with silver.

'What's your name, stranger,' the old man demanded.

Hodgkiss crossed to the bed and held out a hand. 'Edgar
Hodgkiss,' he announced. 'And who's that?' he asked with a
glance back at the short man who was standing at the end of
the bed, obviously displeased at the intrusion.

'Oh him,' said the man in the bed. 'That's Henry Cook,
a neighbour of mine. Take no notice of him. And you know
who I am because you've come to visit me. Am I right?'

'You're Oscar Carpenter. I'm sorry if I came at an inconvenient moment, so if …'

'You mean because you heard him shouting at me. It
would have been inconvenient if you hadn't come just now,
Hodgkiss. You saved me.'

'So what have you come for, Hodgkiss?' Cook demanded
abruptly.

'See what a gentleman he is,' said Carpenter, turning to
Hodgkiss with a shrug of his narrow shoulders. 'See how he

treats my visitors! You ignore him, Hodgkiss. Now, tell me what it is that brings you here?'

Hodgkiss began. 'Well, I was talking to your son about the plan for the eruv ...'

Carpenter flung up his bony arms. 'The eruv! The eruv! Don't talk to me about the eruv.' He paused. 'So, what is it about the eruv you want to talk about?' he demanded.

'Your son mentioned that it runs right through your property and they might have to put up a pole to carry the wire, so I was wondering what ...'

'I won't have it,' the old man burst out. 'No one's putting up poles, not in my front garden. No one! He lives next door,' he said with a nod of his head towards where Cook still hovered at the end of the bed, 'and he doesn't want no poles either.'

'But it's not just the eruv we have to deal with now,' said Cook. 'It's the least of our worries.'

Carpenter nodded furiously. 'No. The eruv is nothing now. Nothing at all. You'll never guess, Hodgkiss, what that collection of crooks is trying to do to us now.'

'By "that collection of crooks" I assume you are talking about Kanundda Council.'

'Of course, who else?'

'Then you must mean their plans to establish a children's playground in your street.'

'Playground shmayground,' the old man spluttered. 'It's a swindle. I won't allow it to happen. Not to my place anyway.'

'I take it you've had a letter from the council about your street being included in the new area suitable for redevelopment for this crazy scam.'

'I haven't seen no letter yet because I've been in this place and nobody tells me nothing,' said the old man, his beard jerking aggressively, 'but Heinrich here,' (another jerk of his head towards the end of the bed) 'he's had the letter. I suppose Michael will bring it when he calls to see me later … if he bothers to call. Of course he'll be tickled pink, Michael will. All he can see is the money. He'll tell me "sell, sell" like some kind of shyster stockbroker.'

'I understand that the agent who's doing the buying is offering pretty fair prices. Well over the odds in many cases,' said Hodgkiss.

'I don't care what he's offering,' the old man said, his voice rising to a shrill squeak. 'No sale. Not now. Not ever.'

'Not ever is a very long time, Oscar,' said Hodgkiss reasonably.

'Not ever is just about right for me, Hodgkiss. And for Harry here, too.'

'I suppose you know that if you refuse to sell, then the council can take steps to force you out. They have power to resume your land in certain circumstances.'

'Yeah! I heard about this resuming thing, but it's not going to happen. Harry here and me, we got a plan. A plan that's sure to work.' The old man laid a sly finger along the side of his nose.

'Really,' said Hodgkiss, interested but not convinced. 'A plan to stop your properties being resumed?'

'Exactly.' Carpenter paused for effect. 'Heritage listing!' he announced impressively. 'We're going to have our places heritage listed then they'll never be able to touch them, not our houses, not our gardens, not anything.'

'And what makes you think that council will agree to heritage listing them?'

'Don't worry about that, Hodgkiss. We're working on it now. We've got people — friends — who know about these things. They say that eight of the houses on our side of the street, where council is planning this playground, they're perfect for heritage listing.'

'And why is that?'

'They were all built by the same fellow who later won some big prize for designing houses. I'd say that's good enough reason, wouldn't you?'

Hodgkiss nodded. 'I'd say it was a pretty good start.'

'But that's not all. All of the foundations were built with sandstone from some local quarry and the timber was all wood cut from local trees and finished at some sawmill that ain't been around for fifty years. And even the gardens; they were all done by some fellow who later became famous as a landscape architect.'

'Sounds like you've really done your homework, but have you discussed the matter with your other neighbours?' Hodgkiss asked. 'Not everyone regards heritage listing as an unalloyed pleasure. It comes with some pretty unreasonable restrictions, you know.'

'Who cares? If they don't like it, to hell with them,' Carpenter said, snapping his fingers. 'This is something very important to us. Anyway, why should any of the others in the street object? Having your house heritage listed is supposed to be good for property values, or so the experts at the Heritage Office told us.'

Hodgkiss laughed humourlessly. 'Yes. They would, wouldn't they? But you ask any real estate agent or anyone with real-life experience in dealing with property on a professional basis and they'll tell you a very different story. Agents know that nine times out of ten when they're showing a prospective purchaser through a house, if they mention the words "heritage listed" that person will be out the door before you can say "white ant."'

'Hey, hey, just whose side are you on, Hodgkiss. Not ours from the sound of it.'

'I'm just not a great fan of heritage listing. Too often it's abused by people who want to see it done for the wrong reasons.'

'What sort of reasons are these?'

'Just to save some worthless pile of bricks so it can't be knocked over for some different sort of development.'

'To stop some developer putting up a block of units, you mean?'

'Precisely. Anyway, I didn't come here to discuss the rights and wrongs of heritage listing.'

'Right, Hodgkiss, so why *did* you come here?'

'I'm doing research for a book I'm planning to write about unsolved crimes in Kanundda. I understand that you might be able to help me about one particular case.'

Hodgkiss heard a sharp intake of breath from the man behind him.

'We don't know nothing about crime, Hodgkiss,' said Oscar Carpenter bluntly.

Hodgkiss continued: 'Mrs Judge seemed fairly sure that you would know something about these people that I'm researching; the Klempner brothers. You must have heard of them.'

Without a word Carpenter reached for the nurses' call button. 'I want you to leave now, Hodgkiss. I've called for the nurse.'

Hodgkiss felt a hand take a tight grip on his right elbow.

He turned. 'There's no need for physical violence, Mr Cook. Your friend here has asked me to leave and I'm leaving, although I must say that this is a most extraordinary reaction.'

'What kind of a reaction were you expecting, Hodgkiss?'

Carpenter demanded. 'You come here asking for information about the Klempners. What do you think we're going to do? Jump for joy. We got nothing to say about them except they were evil and they got what they deserved.'

'You know what happened to them, then?'

'No. Of course we don't know.' The reply came too quickly. 'Why would we know? They just disappeared. Everyone knows that. They were there one day, then they were gone. Who knows where? Who cares?'

'Do you know what happened at the Travellers Inn? Mrs Judge thinks they might have been demanding protection money from the licensee.'

'Yeah. Maybe they were. I wouldn't know, but I wouldn't be surprised either.'

At this point there was a soft knock on the door and the nurse looked in. 'Can I get something for you, Mr Carpenter?'

'No, no, Nurse. It's OK. Everything's OK.'

'You're sure?' She glanced at Hodgkiss, smiled, then withdrew.

'You know about the Klempners then,' Hodgkiss persisted.

'Everyone in the Jewish community knows about them,' said Cook.

'Mrs Judge told me they might have changed their name to Plumber. Did you ever know them under that name?'

Carpenter shook his head. 'We never knew them under that name. Like everyone in our community we knew of the Klempners and like everyone we were very pleased when they disappeared …God be praised.'

'And when they disappeared … how was that. I mean, someone must have noticed that they weren't around any more and reported it to the police.'

Cook shrugged elaborately. 'Why are you asking us? What would we know? We didn't report anything to the police.'

'Well, I know that they *were* reported missing to the police,' Hodgkiss said, knowing that he had no factual basis for this claim, 'which means that someone must have known where they usually lived and that they'd disappeared from there in unusual or suspicious circumstances. There are certain criteria that must be met before police will accept a missing persons report and I believe that such a report was made.'

'They stayed at some hotel in Kylerbrin,' Cook conceded, 'or so we were told at the time. But how long they lived there we wouldn't know. They might have some kind of record or visitors' book still at the hotel.'

'Hardly likely. Not after all this time,' said Hodgkiss, nevertheless making a mental note to inquire at the Travellers Inn about the existence of any old records.

'Well, there's nothing else we can tell you about those people, except that everyone was glad to see the back of them.'

'But why did everyone assume they'd disappeared. That's what I don't understand. Why didn't you think that they'd just moved on; gone to live somewhere else?'

Cook and Carpenter looked at each other but said nothing.

Cook turned, looked steadily at Hodgkiss. 'How should we know?' he asked. 'Everyone just said they'd disappeared … vanished … gone. We didn't pay much notice how people knew it. We were just very glad about it.'

'Have you any idea how long they lived in the area?'

Carpenter frowned. 'No idea. Maybe a month or two. Maybe a little longer.'

'And what in particular was it about them that lead you to believe they were evil? Everyone I've spoken to so far tells me the same thing — how wicked they were. But what else had they done apart from this stand-over business with the licensee of the Travellers Inn?'

'Mr Hodgkiss,' said Carpenter with a massive display of patience, 'you are asking us to discuss matters that we will not talk about. I do not wish to be rude to a stranger but there you are. End of story. Now, if you will excuse us, Mr Cook here, and I, we have other matters to discuss.'

Hodgkiss headed for the door. 'Very well, gentlemen. But I've a strong feeling that we will resume this conversation before long.'

*   *   *

When he arrived home Hodgkiss went straight to his room and took from the top drawer of his desk the envelope that Jan Campbell-Jones had left in the Burke's letterbox the previous day.

At first the contents appeared disappointing. The envelope contained only two typed sheets stapled together and a single page photocopied from an old newspaper which Hodgkiss had never seen or heard of.

The page was copied from an issue of the Northside Gazette dated November 24, 1938. A circle had been drawn in pencil pen around a story near the bottom of the page.

The story was headed —

POLICE INQUIRING

FOR ALIEN BROTHERS

Police are anxious to interview two foreign nationals believed to be living in the Kylerbrin area.

The two persons being sought are known as Hans and Fritz Klempner, believed to be brothers.

The inquiries are being made following complaints by

certain German-speaking immigrant residents in the St James community.

The complainants are claiming that the persons in question have been behaved in a menacing manner and issuing threats to residents of this area. It is also claimed that the persons have been responsible for some destruction of property in and around the St James shopping centre.

Information provided to police so far has not enabled them to locate the two men but inquiries are proceeding.

Hodgkiss was about to put down the sheet when another article at the top of the page caught his eye. It was headed —

NAZI SUPPORTERS

ATTACK JEWISH SHOPS

In an extraordinary outbreak of co-ordinated violence, mobs of pro-Nazi youths, encouraged by high ranking Nazi military offi-cers went on an orgy of violence and destruction throughout Germany and parts of Austria on the night of November 9/10.

Thousands of synagogues were destroyed by fire and a large but unknown number of Jewish citizens were arrested. Their fate is still not known although it is believed many have already been sent to forced labour camps.

In particular the premises of Jewish businessmen were attacked and their windows smashed leaving huge quantities of broken glass littering the street of all major cities and even small towns and villages.

Already many Jewish businessmen and their families are believed to be fleeing the country to join the many thousands who had already fled Germany ahead of the violence.

Frowning thoughtfully, Hodgkiss put down the page and picked up the two sheets stapled together.

The first sheet was covered in closely-spaced text on a typewriter with several poorly aligned letters.

It was headed –

Report of Community Welfare Officer Kingston on public meeting at St James Masonic Hall, November 8, 1938.

In accordance with the directions of the Town Clerk I attended a public meeting held in the St James Masonic Hall beginning at 7 p.m.

The meeting was well attended with about 120 people present, mostly members of a local religious community.

It was called following reports of threats of violence against some members of the community and their wives and families. These threats were issued by unnamed persons at present resident at an hotel at Kylerbrin and although none of these threats have been carried out the very presence of these individual and of others who are supporting them in their conduct has become such a cause of concern locally that the meeting was called to bring the activities of these people to public notice.

Among those present at the meeting were three police officers from local stations, including a senior officer from North Sydney.

Also present were two members of parliament whose constituencies cover this area.

The chairman of the meeting was a local identity Mr Tischler. It was also Mr Tischler who caused advertisements to be placed in the Northside Gazette advertising the meeting.

Mr Tischler said that members of his community had deemed it necessary to call the meeting to bring to notice the threats that certain persons, not present at the meeting, had issued to them. These threats included threats of physical violence and demands for money which had no basis in any sort of legal transaction.

Mr Tischler described these demands for money as protection for their businesses. He said that he had been told that if he did not pay sums of money then his business, an upholstery workshop on Spring Vale Road, St James, would suffer damage.

There was more comment along these lines when a second member of the local community addressed the meeting later.

Mr Heinrich Koch, who keeps a café in Spring Vale Road, St James, told the meeting that he had been threatened by the persons referred to earlier who were not present at the meeting. He told the meeting these persons had told him that his business would suffer if he failed to pay a fixed sum of money each week. In this context the Mr Koch referred to an alleged incident, recently reported upon, at the Travellers Inn on the Northern Highway at Kylerbrin.

Mr Koch concluded by telling the meeting that he had been told that if the money demanded was not paid then every window in his place of business would be smashed as would the windows of all other members of the community who were in business in the area.

Another three speakers from the body of the hall were heard who contributed little that had not already been expressed by Messrs Tischler and Koch.

The two members of parliament both spoke very briefly. They both expressed the view that the threats issued were un-Australian and that they were appalled. Neither recommended a specific course of action that might help to resolve the situation.

Hodgkiss put down the papers. Typical, he thought. Useless politicians. And the local council apparently was not greatly concerned since they sent only some junior clerk to take notes and report back.

There was nothing to show that they actually took any practical action to head off trouble.

Just then Esme tapped on his bedroom door, a large manila envelope in one hand. 'Donald dropped this off earlier while you were out. I think it's something to do with your research about unsolved crime. That missing persons business you were telling him about.'

Hodgkiss rose. 'Thank you, my dear,' he said taking the envelope. 'Now let's see what he has managed to dig out from his old files. From the feel of the envelope it seems that his digging has not been particularly productive.' He sat down again at his desk then turned to call after Esme as she headed back to the kitchen. 'I suppose a cup of tea would be out of the question.'

'Out on the deck in five minutes,' came the reply.

While the envelope may have promised little in quantity it proved rich in content.

The first document Hodgkiss drew from the envelope was a missing persons report written by a police sergeant.

The sergeant recorded that a Mr Irish of Kylerbrin had attended the Crestwood Police Station at about 8.15 p.m. on November 15 and reported the disappearance of Hans and Fritz Klempner, brothers, who had been resident for more than two weeks at the Travellers Inn, Northern Road, Kylerbrin, where he was the licensee.

Mr Irish stated that the Klempner brothers had been absent from their lodgings for three days now.

He had stressed that his concern arose from the fact that they had paid for their accommodation for a month in advance and he thought that they were unlikely to leave the hotel without attempting to reclaim the credit balance of their board and lodging. They were not that kind of people.

Mr Irish said he had decided to make the report because they had left behind several large suitcases and items deposited in the hotel's safe. He did not wish to be encumbered with these items and possibly held resposible for them at some later date.

When it was pointed out to Mr Irish that the Klempners had not been absent from their accommodation for more than a few days Mr Irish made it quite clear that while this was true, nevertheless he did not expect them to return.

When questioned on his reason for this view he would only say that they had both made themselves extremely unpopular during the time they had lived in the district and if they had got 'what was coming to them' then Mr Irish, for one, would not be at all surprised or upset.

He would not elaborate on this statement although pressed to do so.

The Sergeant then made a brief reference to a recent incident at the Travellers Inn when, it was alleged, the brothers had engaged in a dispute with the licensee of that place and persuaded him to open his safe and pay over a sum of money.

Hodgkiss put down the report.

He decided that obviously it would be worth his while to investigate whether or not Mr Irish was still in the land of the living and available for interview.

He turned his attention to the only other document in the envelope, a single sheet from an occurrence pad, completed in copperplate script.

November 11, 1938. Reports of serious disturbances in the shopping centre at St James. A number of local businesses were vandalised, windows were smashed leaving large quantities of dangerous broken class on footpaths and roadways. Arrangements have been made for these to be cleaned up. All the business owners whose premises were vandalised have been contacted and they are now taking action to secure their premises. It is feared that in many cases those responsible for the acts of vandalism also looted items from the premises attacked. There is an obvious need for serious action in this matter to establish the identity of the vandals because those whose premises were the victims of attacks seem to have just fear that their will be a repetition of these acts.

It is worth noting that very recently there was a well-attended public meeting at the Masonic Hall at St James when local traders and other businessmen complained that they had been the subject of threats of violence against themselves and against their property.

Constables Smith and Roberts have been assigned to take statements from all those affected by the acts of vandalism as well as from a number of residents of the area who were eyewitnesses to these attacks.

Hodgkiss sighed. *Kristallnacht in St James.* What a depressing thought. And the very next night after the same thing had happened in Germany and Austria, except over there it was on a truly frightening scale.

He returned the papers to the envelope rose and headed for the deck, meaning to join Esme for afternoon tea.

But the cordless phone in the hall rang as he walked past. With an impatient snort he paused and raised the receiver.

'Yes?!' he snapped.

'Is that Edgar Hodgkiss?'

'Yes, this is Hodgkiss.'

'Sorry to bother you, Mr Hodgkiss. This is Michael Carpenter. We spoke the other day. Is there any chance of seeing you this afternoon? It's rather urgent.'

''Is it about the eruv?' Hodgkiss asked.

'No. It's not about the eruv. Things have moved on from the eruv.'

'Moved on. What does that mean?' Hodgkiss demanded peevishly.

'Look, Mr Hodgkiss, it's not something I can talk about over the phone. Can you come and see me? Or can I visit you, or meet you somewhere?'

I suppose so,' Hodgkiss conceded grudgingly.

'Fine. Do you know the little park in Open Creek Road? Could you meet me there in half an hour?'

'Yes. I suppose so. Half an hour.'

Hodgkiss disconnected the call and continued on his way to the back deck where Esme was waiting, seated at the redwood table with two mugs filled with black tea.

'Who was that on the phone?' she asked.

'That was a fellow called Michael Carpenter. He wants to meet me in half an hour at St. James. Would you mind driving me there, Esme? It's not far and whatever he wants to talk about shouldn't take long.'

'But Dad, I've got to start dinner' she protested.

'It won't be the end of the world if dinner's a few minutes late. We won't starve, will we?'

Esme sighed. 'No, I suppose not.' She sipped her tea. 'What's it about? Isn't Michael Carpenter the fellow who wrote to the paper in support of the eruv?'

Hodgkiss nodded. 'Yes, but he may have changed his mind, going on what he said just now.'

'Oh. What did he say?'

'He just said something about things having moved on from the eruv.'

'And what was that supposed to mean?'

'Really, Esme, I've no idea,' Hodgkiss snapped. 'That's why I'm going to meet him. He said he didn't want to talk about it on the phone, whatever *it* is.'

Esme parked her small beige sedan adjacent to the neatly-kept well-shaded park. A late model Mercedes stood nearby and in the park a middle-aged man sat on a brightly-painted bench near a slippery-dip. A manila envelope rested on the seat beside him.

'Looks like your friend's already here,' Esme observed. 'You're like a couple of spies meeting to hand over the secret plans.'

'I think that is rather over-dramatizing the situation, Esme. Still, I suppose it may prove to be an interesting meeting. Young Carpenter certainly sounded very much on edge over something or other.' He climbed out onto the unmade footpath and turned. 'I shouldn't be very long at all.'

Esme held up an ornately bound copy of Little Dorrit. 'Don't worry about me, Dad. I brought something to read.'

Michael Carpenter stood up as Hodgkiss approached. 'Thanks for coming, Hodgkiss. I hope I didn't interrupt anything. It's just that I've discovered something that you may be interested in for your research. By the way, Dad told me that you visited him this morning. You know he wasn't very pleased about it.'

Hodgkiss nodded. 'Yes. And his neighbour Henry Cook was with him when I arrived. He wasn't particularly pleased to see me either.'

They say down side by side on the bench. 'Now, what's this about, Carpenter?' Hodgkiss asked.

Carpenter looked down at the envelope. 'Before Dad went into the nursing home he drew up a continuing power of attorney and gave me authority to deal with all his affairs.'

Hodgkiss nodded. 'And now he wants to tear it up … revoke it. Is that what's happened?'

Carpenter shrugged. 'Yes. The silly, stubborn old man'

'And did he … tear it up?'

'No. Not yet. I haven't taken it back to the nursing home yet. I only just found it.'

'But you *will* take it too him. He has every right to revoke it.'

'Oh yes. I wouldn't argue with that. He's in full possession of all his faculties … and then some.' He hesitated. 'I was going to take it back to him this afternoon but when I opened the desk where he keeps all his private papers I came across something else while I was looking for the power of attorney document.'

'I take it your father keeps his private papers under lock and key,' Hodgkiss said.

'Oh, yes. He was always very particular about keeping his desk locked, but he had to give me the key to get the power of attorney document.'

'And this other item you found. Was it some form of personal recollection … a diary, perhaps?'

Carpenter looked up sharply. 'What makes you think that?'

Hodgkiss nodded thoughtfully. 'I just formed the impression from speaking with him that your father and his father, and very likely his neighbour, Mr Cook, are both people whose families have a very interesting past. No doubt they could tell some fascinating tales if they felt inclined to do so. It occurred to me that there may well be some formal record kept by the families relating to these matters. Also that envelope looks about the right size to hold a smallish, thickish book.'

'You're not wrong, Mr Hodgkiss. This item I found by accident was a diary, or rather a series of old diaries.'

'Dating back to the thirties?'

Carpenter nodded. 'Yes. It looks like my grand-father then my father kept a pretty detail record of events. Grandfather started writing these entries before he and grandmother and Dad escaped from Germany.'

'Then it must be an absolutely absorbing document. That was a most dramatic and terrible time in human history.'

'I've no doubt you're right. But the problem is that my German is not very good and I've made no effort to read any of them. It would be a major operation with my limited vocabulary. Of course I understand a few words here and there, but overall I've no idea what's in them.'

'And for how long did your grandfather keep the diaries?'

'Almost daily until he died which was not long after the war ended. But I suspect that you may be more interested in the earlier years, if you can find someone to help with the translation.'

'I'm quite sure I would be extremely interested, partic-ularly in the year 1938. Did your grandfather make many entries during that year?'

'He certainly did. In fact in 1938 he made entries almost every day; very complete and very detailed entries by the look of them.'

Hodgkiss smiled grimly. 'Yes. I expect they would be. There would be many matters that occurred during those months that would have concerned him very much. It was a difficult year not only there but all around the world.'

'No doubt about that, Mr Hodgkiss.'

'As I mentioned when we spoke yesterday, I am carrying out research on unsolved crimes in the early days of this area. Is there anything in this diary of your grandfather's that would help me in my research? In particularly I refer to the mysterious disappearance of two brothers by the name of Klempner. From what you've read of the diaries does that name appear anywhere?'

Carpenter nodded gravely. 'Yes. In fact there are several references to those two. Although I can't read what it is he's written about them, the name Klempner appears frequently throughout the entries for 1938.'

'I fancy that even if you could have read them none would have been very complementary.'

'No. Probably not.' He hesitated. 'Anyway, I've brought the volume for 1938 with me. Would you like to look at it now, or you could take it home if you wish. I've no doubt you'll take good care of it and I'm sure Dad wouldn't mind at all.'

'That's very generous of you, Michael. I'll take it home with me if you don't mind and make a thorough study of it, providing of course I can find a reliable translator. Obviously it would have to be someone who was the soul of discretion. Anything in the diary that I decide is appropriate for use in my book, if indeed any book ever sees the light of day, I will discuss first with both you and your father, particularly any material which may reflect upon your family or your connections.'

'I'd appreciate that, Mr Hodgkiss. When you've read it we can talk about it then. I suspect that the diary will disclose quite a deal of criminal activity, but no doubt those responsible will be long gone from the land of the living.'

'No doubt. My son-in-law is a detective sergeant of police

presently stationed at Crestwood, so he will be able to make a judgment on that if one is required. He has already, at my request, unearthed some very interesting material on the subject, particularly with reference to the Klempner brothers and two members of the Jewish community at that time; folk by the name of Koch and Tischler.'

Carpenter raised his eyes and looked steadily at Hodgkiss. 'Mr Hodgkiss. You should know that the German word for Carpenter is Tischler and Koch is German for Cook.'

Hodgkiss nodded. 'And another local family, the Judges, changed their name from Richter.'

'Same idea,' said Carpenter.

'Thank you for that information. It means that the puzzle is now just a fraction less complicated.'

'Which particular puzzle was that, Mr Hodgkiss? There seems to me to be quite a number of unsolved puzzles at the moment.'

'I am referring to the puzzle of what became of the Klempner brothers.'

'So you think they died about that time, the time they were supposed to have disappeared in late 1938?'

Hodgkiss nodded. 'Undoubtedly they died, and about that time. But I was referring to the other puzzle; what became of them ... or rather, of their bodies.'

Carpenter's eyebrows arched. 'You think you know where they are buried, then?'

Hodgkiss nodded somberly. 'I believe so. But before committing myself I would like to know what this has to say on the subject, if anything.' He held up the diary.

'I'd be very interested to know too. Dad has never been at all forthcoming about practically every aspect of our family history. I've asked often enough about what became of other members of the family — I know he had two brothers — but he refuses absolutely to talk about them or about anything to do with his family. I gave up asking years ago.'

Hodgkiss tucked the diary under an arm and held out a hand.

Carpenter took the hand then both men headed for the roadway where their cars were parked.

*   *   *

'What have you got there, Dad?' Esme asked with a glance at the diary as Hodgkiss climbed into the passenger's seat.

'This, I hope, contains the key to the puzzle I have been working on. This is old Oscar Carpenter's father's diary for the year 1938. Apparently he was a most enthusiastic and thorough diarist.'

Esme frowned. 'I don't know if I like the idea of you reading someone else's personal diary, Dad. That just doesn't seem right to me.'

''Well, his grandson seems to think it's all right so I would say that makes it all right, wouldn't you?' He settled the book in his lap, opened the cover then turned over the first page.

'Of course it's all written in German so I'll have to find someone who can translate it.'

'Why don't you take it back to that old fellow you visited in the nursing home. It was his father that wrote it, wasn't it?' Esme suggested.

Hodgkiss thought, then nodded approval. 'It was indeed. An excellent suggestion, Esme. No doubt there will be material in the diary that will require elaboration and Oscar may be in a position to fill in any blanks. May we go home now, please Esme, so I can make the necessary arrangements to call on him?'

'Just one thing that really puzzles me, Dad,' said Esme, starting the car, slipping the selector into Drive and pulling away. 'Why do you think Mr Carpenter gave you his grandfather's diary to read? That seems really odd to me.'

Hodgkiss smiled. 'That is a most perceptive question, my dear. It is one that has been exercising my mind ever since he suggested I borrow it. I have formed a provisional view on the matter and it is a view that does not reflect great credit on young Carpenter.'

'You mean you think that somehow he's selling his family out; that by giving his grandfather's diary to you he thinks that things are likely to work out somehow to his own advantage and not his father's.'

'That is an irresistible conclusion in the circumstances. Not only that, it is apparent that he is using me to achieve some ends of his own, very likely unworthy ends. That is why your suggestion that I should seek Carpenter senior's assistance in the translation is so attractive. Old Oscar should be kept in the loop with everything that is going on.'

'But if what we think turns out to be right and young Carpenter is trying to do the wrong thing by his Dad, then he won't be all that chuffed if he finds out that you let his Dad know that he handed over the diary for you to read.'

Hodgkiss shrugged. 'Not my problem, Esme. Besides, I have no brief for young Carpenter and I am quite happy to let any blame fall where it will, that is if there is ultimately any blame to fall anywhere.

'Besides, young Carpenter must have at least considered the possibility that I would approach his father for a translation, or at least some other German-speaking local who would very likely know his father and bring the matter to his attention.' Hodgkiss shook his head. 'There is no doubt that Carpenter junior's motives in giving me this diary are highly troubling and suspect.'

Esme turned the small car into the driveway at the side of the Burke's home, pressed the button on the remote to raise the garage door and drove in.

When they climbed the shallow flight of steps to the back deck, meaning to enter the house through the sliding door to the family room, they were surprised to find a short, bald man sitting in Hodgkiss's favourite deck chair.

The man clambered awkwardly to his feet.

'Mr Cook,' said Hodgkiss. 'Or should I saw Herr Koch.'

Cook was unperturbed 'Either will do, Hodgkiss.'

'Very well, Mr Cook. Now, what can I do for you?'

'First of all you can give me that,' said Cook jabbing a finger at the diary which Hodgkiss was carrying in his left hand.

'And why should I do that?' Hodgkiss asked quietly.

'Because it doesn't belong to you. That's why.'

Hodgkiss nodded. 'Yes, that's true. But it doesn't belong to you either, does it?'

'It belongs to my friend and he wants it back.'

'I can well believe he does as I've no doubt it contains material that he would prefer never saw the light of day.'

'What's in the diary is none of your business, Hodgkiss.'

'I wouldn't argue with that. But then the question arises, "whose business is it?" If, as I suspect, the diary contains material that would be evidence of a crime then it may be someone else's business would it not ... the police for example?'

Cook flashed indignantly. 'It contains nothing of the sort. There was no crime committed ... nothing that any sane person would call a crime.'

'Perhaps,' Hodgkiss conceded. 'But your idea of what was a crime and how the police may view it could be entirely different.'

'You don't know what you're talking about, Hodgkiss. Do you know how old that diary is? How long ago those things were done? What in the diary could possibly be of any interest to the police now after so many years?'

'You may be right, Mr Cook, but there's really only one way to find out. As you know my main interest is in finding out about the disappearance of the Klempner brothers. I suppose you know that there was a missing persons report filed on them at the time, so there is no doubt that the police have a legitimate interest in the matter. They like to tidy things up … close cases, no matter how old.'

The old man pleaded. 'But, Hodgkiss, it was all so long ago.'

'Old crimes cast long shadows,' Hodgkiss quoted piously.

'But I tell you — there…was…no…crime…committed.'

'Then you can tell me, can you, what became of the Klempners?'

Cook shook his head vigorously. 'I can tell you nothing,' he said stubbornly. 'Now, I want that diary.' He held out a hand.

Hodgkiss hesitated then nodded. 'Very well. I will return it.'

'Unread!' Cook insisted.

'Yes. But first I'd like to know how you get here so soon. We left Michael Carpenter in the park only ten minutes ago at the most.'

Cook grinned. 'Oscar realised as soon as he gave Michael the key to fetch his power of attorney document from the desk that he would very likely find the diary. He rang Michael who told him that had found it and that he intended to pass it on to you to assist you with your research.'

Hodgkiss shook his head. 'That was an extraordinary decision on Michael's part and, as my daughter Esme here and I believe, it was a decision made with very dubious motives.'

'Michael is a bad son,' Cook said gravely. 'I have known the Tischlers for most of my life and I know what a disappointment Michael is to his father. He is interested only in one thing — money. He would sell the house tomorrow if he had a good offer. He would sell his mother if she was still alive. And her mother too if he could get a good price.'

'And of course he has had a good offer on the house now, has he not? A very good offer.'

Cook nodded. 'That is why this matter is more urgent than ever. He is eager to sell. Oscar heard of it from me after all of us in the street received the offer from the estate agent. He spoke to Michael who said he would sell and Oscar said at once he would revoke the power of attorney. Anyway, when Michael told Oscar that he intended to give you the diary Oscar asked me to come here to persuade you to return it without first reading it.'

Hodgkiss nodded. 'Well, that clears that up. Here. Have the thing back.'

Cook took the diary and placed it under an arm. 'I suppose there are some things you would still like to know for your research.'

'Just one thing really: how did the Klempners die?'

'Is that all?'

'Yes. I suppose that must be something of a relief to you. No doubt you thought I would also want to know what became of them after they were dead.'

Cook nodded. 'Yes. I thought you'd certainly want to ask

that. But you don't? Why is that?'

Hodgkiss paused for effect. 'Because I know that … where they are now.'

Cook's jaw dropped. 'But how would you know, Hodgkiss? Nobody knows that but Oscar and I. Not even Michael knows.'

'No. Michael wouldn't know. Probably he wasn't even born then, was he?'

Cook ignored the question. 'When I return this to Oscar I'll tell him what you say. He may agree to tell you what you want to know about how the Klempners died. I'll call you.'

They shook hands. Cook made a polite bow in Esme's direction, then was gone.

Esme unlocked the sliding aluminium door to the family room and Hodgkiss followed her through the house to the kitchen where she lit the gas stove with an old-fashioned flint gun then put on the kettle to boil.

Hodgkiss slid into his usual side of the built-in pine breakfast nook while Esme put tea into an old battered aluminium teapot with red Bakelite handles. Then she turned and leaned against the bench beside the sink.

'Dad. Why did you tell that Mr Cook that you knew where the Klempners are now … where they're buried? That's what you meant, isn't it?' she asked.

Hodgkiss frowned. 'Esme. Don't ask ridiculous questions.'

'Well,' Esme snapped, 'I wouldn't *have* to ask ridiculous questions if you didn't make ridiculous statements. You've no idea where they're buried … have you? I bet that was just bluff.'

'Bluff! Why should I try to bluff him?'

'If Donald was here he'd say you were just showing off … grandstanding … making a big fellow of yourself.'

'Yes, no doubt that's exactly what Donald *would* say. And

as usual he would be wrong. But is that really what you think, that I'm only bluffing?'

Esme shook her head. 'I really don't know. But if you *do* know where those two are buried don't you have a duty to do something about it. What if they really were murdered? That means that there's a murderer somewhere who has got away with it.'

'Not necessarily. It's so long ago that the murderer is very likely dead, too, by now.'

'Maybe,' Esme conceded. 'But maybe not. He could still be alive. He could still be out there somewhere.'

'Then he'd be a very old murderer by now, wouldn't he? And he would have committed the crime when he was a very young man. I think it's most unlikely that he'd be still around. But his family might be.'

'Is that what you're worried about? Any family that's still alive?'

'It's certainly worth considering, don't you think? But there's no point in discussing this any further, not until we know how the Klempners died and if there was actually a crime committed.'

Esme nodded. 'Yes. I suppose you're right, Dad. But is it a crime to bury someone without all of the usual arrangements? I mean, you've got to have a death certificate, an undertaker's got to be involved, and ...'

'Yes, Esme. You're absolutely right. If they were buried without all of the proper requirements being met that would be an offence against some law or other, but I think we are dealing with something rather more serious than that.'

The kettle began to whistle and Esme turned and began to pour the boiling water into the teapot. Hodgkiss got up, crossed the kitchen, opened a cupboard on the wall above the microwave and took down a china biscuit barrel with a silverplate lid and a handle in the form of a dragon.

Esme took a small wooden tray from a cupboard beside the sink and set out on it two mugs and a wooden bowl containing raw sugar.

'We might as well have it on the deck,' she said. 'I don't expect Mr Cook or his friends are likely to call back very soon.'

Hodgkiss raised an eyebrow. 'If at all.'

*   *   *

But Hodgkiss's scepticism was soon proved baseless.

The cordless phone in the hall rang just before nine the following morning.

Donald, who was passing the phone on his way to the garage to set off for duty at the nearby Crestwood Police Station, scooped up the handset. He listened attentively as he walked the length of the hall the handset pressed to an ear. In the kitchen he paused and set down the instrument in front of Hodgkiss who was sitting in the breakfast nook, the morning paper spread open before him.

'It's someone called Oscar something-or-other,' he said *sotto voce*. 'I didn't quite catch the other name.'

Hodgkiss picked up the phone. 'Yes, Mr Carpenter,' he said.

'Mr Hodgkiss,' came the thick German voice. 'I thank you for returning my property to me. That was very honourable of you. Also it was very wicked of my son to pass it on to you in the first place. For this he will be punished.' He paused. 'My friend Cook has told me that I should satisfy your curiosity about the death of the Klempner brothers.'

'I would appreciate that, Mr Carpenter, but only if you think it appropriate,' said Hodgkiss.

Carpenter chuckled. 'If I did not think it appropriate I would not tell you a thing. I would not be ringing. Mr Cook also said something that I found very interesting. He said that you told him you knew where the Klempners were to be found. Is that true?'

'Do you mean is it true that I told that to Mr Cook, or that I know where the Klempners are ... resting?

'The second one. Where they are now.'

'Of course I cannot be positive because I was not there when they were put under the ground. But the indications are so suggestive that there is little doubt in my mind about it. But we do not wish to discuss this over the telephone, do we?'

'No, we certainly do not. Can you come to visit me again?'

'Certainly. When would it suit you?'

'There's no point in delaying. Can you come today? This afternoon perhaps.'

'I should think so. I will have to ask my daughter about it because I do not drive a car.' He glanced at Esme who had been following the conversation. She nodded her head with little enthusiasm. 'She says it's all right. Two thirty, then?'

Hodgkiss nodded then cut the call.

'Good thing I had nothing on this afternoon,' Esme observed. 'I really do wish that you'd learn to drive, Dad. It'd save us both a lot of bother.'

'Esme, I have managed to muddle through my sixty eight years without holding a driver's licence. I see no reason why I should put the welfare of the motoring public at risk by acquiring one at this time of my life.'

Esme shook her head. 'No, you wouldn't,' she said crossly.

'It's always me or Donald who's got to drive you here or there at a moment's notice.'

'Really, Esme, if you find it inconvenient to drive me a few kilometers for what I think is quite an important meeting, well, there is such a thing as a taxi.'

'I'm not having you paying for a taxi when there's a perfectly good motor car in our garage.'

At exactly two thirty Esme parked her car outside the Rosemount rest home. 'Do you want me to come in with you?' she asked. 'I brought something with me to read so I wouldn't mind waiting in the car,' she added.

'I really don't know how long I'll be,' said Hodgkiss. 'I don't know what Carpenter has in mind, but I can't imagine that it would take more than half an hour for him to tell me whatever it is that's on his mind.'

So Esme pressed the recline lever on the side of her seat and settled down comfortably behind the steering wheel to read while Hodgkiss climbed out onto the nature strip and headed for the entry at the side of the rambling building.

The same cheerful nurse was sitting, studying at the nurse's station in the entry hall. She looked up, smiling. 'Mr Hodgkiss, isn't it? Mr Carpenter and Mr Cook are expecting you. Will you come this way?'

Hodgkiss followed the nurse's youthful figure with interest as she lead the way down the same corridor to the same door where she tapped lightly with her knuckles.

The door was pulled open at once and Cook stood, waiting, grim faced. He stepped to one side. 'Come in, Hodgkiss, and let me tell you right from the beginning that I do not think this meeting is such a good idea. I've told him'– a toss of his head to where Oscar Carpenter lay propped up in his bed — 'that he's crazy to trust you.'

He heaved his shoulders 'But what can I do? What am I? A silly old Jew, that's what.'

Carpenter chipped in. 'Take no notice of him, Hodgkiss. I asked you to come and see me, not him.' He waved an angry hand in Cook's direction. 'And if you don't like it you can clear off. You don't have to stay.'

'Of course I have to stay. How can I trust you not to let your silly wagging tongue run away. In all your life you never knew when to stop talking, why should you change now?'

'Don't talk rubbish you old fool. Hodgkiss, here, he knows what's happened so what's the point of ...'

Cook barked. 'What does he know? He knows nothing.' He turned to Hodgkiss. 'You say you know things. What do you know? Tell me.'

Hodgkiss shook his head. 'I don't *know* anything; but I have a pretty good idea of what became of those two men, the Klempners.'

'Everyone knows what became of them,' Cook snapped. 'They disappeared ... vanished. So what else do you know?'

'Nothing much,' Hodgkiss admitted. He tried a wry smile. 'But I'm willing and eager to learn.'

Cook turned to Carpenter, arms spread. 'What did I tell you? What does he know? Nothing. That's what he knows.'

'Heinrich, never mind what he knows or doesn't know. *I* know what *I* know and that is that he has earned the right to be told ... what happened there that night. He's an honest man and he has an interest in the matter. Besides, I think he could make more than a guess about where to find those two now.' He turned to Hodgkiss. 'Am I right, Hodgkiss?'

'It's true that it would be nothing more than a guess, but I think it would be very close to the mark. Anyway, since your friend here, Mr Cook, seems so anxious about you telling me the history of the matter I am quite prepared to turn around and go home and let the matter rest. My daughter is still waiting outside in the car.'

'You'll do nothing of the sort, Hodgkiss. Never mind what he says. The fact is I've made up my mind that you should have the information you want for your research about those missing men. But I've got one condition for telling you.'

'Oh, and what is that?'

'I want you to promise me that when you write up this research of yours, your book or whatever it is, that you won't say where it is that you think that the Klempners are buried. That's all I ask.'

'I've got no problem with that. My research is about unsolved crimes. Now. if you are going to tell me that no crime was committed ...'

Carpenter shook his head vigourously. 'No, I wouldn't say that. There was certainly a crime. Or that's what the law would call it today.'

Hodgkiss nodded and settled comfortably in a tubular-steel framed chair beside the bed. 'Now may we talk about that diary and what happened back then — in nineteen-thirty-eight? In November, wasn't it?'

Carpenter reached over to a metal locker beside the bed, pulled open a draw and took out the diary. 'It all started before November. And earlier than nineteen-thirty-eight.' He turned to Cook who was standing at the end of the bed. 'When would you say it really started Heinrich?'

'It started as soon as they arrived in the country, that's when,' said Cook. 'In nineteen-thirty six. Probably even earlier than that. That's when they started making trouble for us ... for all of us.'

'You're referring to the Klempner brothers. Who were they? Hodgkiss asked.

'Germans,' said Carpenter. 'Nazi sympathisers.'

'If they were Nazi sympathisers why did they come to Australia then — before the war? I thought it was only those who the Nazis were persecuting who left Germany then.'

Carpenter shook his head. 'Not so. The Klempners, they left because they had to leave. They were common criminals as well as Jew-haters.'

'If they were criminals it's a wonder they had permission to enter this country. In those days our migration officials were pretty particular about who they let in. They could have been kept out by using the dictation test.'

'Well, whatever the reason there were no problems for the Klempners. Of course in Germany they had their criminal friends, influential friends in the Nazi party who could have provided for them forged identity papers, money, everything.'

Hodgkiss nodded. 'So they began to throw their weight around among your community when they arrived out here. Is that it?'

'They did more than throw their weight around. They gathered a gang of thugs about them to prey upon us Jewish refugees. You must understand, Hodgkiss, that we were not all that popular with Australians when first we came to your country. The Klempners used to tell anyone who would listen to them, things about us that were quite untrue, and there were some people who were happy to believe anything they said against us. Oh, they could sound so very convincing. Then of course there were always articles in the papers from the Continent that were printed specially to make things look bad for us and many people were too ready to believe it all.

'All lies,' said Cook.

'So the Klempners stood over us, demanded money, made some of us work for them in their businesses for very little money. They became very wealthy men.'

'But, if they were so powerful why would they bother standing over the licensee of a suburban hotel?' Hodgkiss asked. 'Surely he would have been very small fry. Not big enough to be worth their while.'

Carpenter smiled grimly. 'They happened to be staying there at the time. But it was never too much trouble for them to bully or extort money from one of us.'

'Then the licensee, Mr Irish, he wasn't Irish at all.'

'Mr Irish wasn't even English. But he was a good man. He tried to stand up to them and look what happened to him?'

'I understand they beat him up and made him open the safe and hand over money … money he never really owed. Protection money.'

Carpenter nodded. 'He'd've been lucky if that was all they did. After they took his money then they took away his daughter, a lovely girl, and put her to work in one of their … establishments in the city.'

'Swine,' Cook put in softly.

'I think I'm beginning to understand,' Hodgkiss muttered.

'No, Hodgkiss,' said Cook, angrily. 'You don't understand. How could you ever understand? You have no idea what it was like for us in those days; what they did to us and our families. And we could do nothing.'

'Couldn't you have gone to the police?'

'The police! What use were they. These men, they were rich, they had the policemen in their pockets. Beside the policemen weren't very fond of us either. They didn't trust us because of all the bad things that were said about us … all the sneering and the names people called us. Even here was not a good place for us to live.'

'But better than Germany,' said Carpenter softly.

Cook sighed. 'Yes. It was better than Germany. At least we did not die like rats in a gas chamber like so many others, so many of our family and our friends.'

'But Hodgkiss here, he did not come to listen to our old horror stories.' said Carpenter. 'He came to find out what happened to the two Klempners. How they died. You still want to know that, don't you, Hodgkiss?'

Hodgkiss nodded.

'Very well, then.' Carpenter opened the diary. 'I'll read you a couple of entries that my father wrote.' He reached behind him and from under a pillow drew out a pair of reading glasses. He hooked them over his ears then settled them precariously on the end of his nose.

'Did my son read you out anything that is written here?' he said, holding up the diary.

Hodgkiss shook his head. 'He told me he couldn't read much German.'

Carpenter's eyebrows rose and he glanced towards Cook. 'Is that what he told you?' He shrugged and turned his attention to the diary.

Hodgkiss saw the old man's eyes, magnified by the glasses, move across the page. He blinked several times as if to clear his vision.

'Oscar, you do not need to read this stuff,' said Cook. 'No one needs to hear it.'

'He's right,' said Hodgkiss, rising. 'I don't want you to read out word for word from your father's diary. That's not why I came here.'

Cook turned and snapped. 'Then what have you come here for, Hodgkiss, if not for that? You're just making trouble.

You're causing pain to my friend.'

'Yes, I can see that,' said Hodgkiss rising.

Carpenter hold up a hand. 'No. Sit down, Hodgkiss. Stay where you are. You came here to find out what became of the damned Klempners and I don't want you to leave without finding out at least that much to put in your book.'

'But I don't even know yet if I'll write a book,' Hodgkiss protested. 'I haven't done much research at all so far. Certainly not enough for a book on the subject.'

'Never mind,' said Carpenter. 'And sit down.' He licked a finger and began to thumb through pages of the old diary.

'Here's the part I want to read. I haven't looked at these pages in fifty years.' He paused, then read:

Thursday, November 10, 1938. Today came into the shop Hans Klempner. There was at the time no customers with me, not that it would have mattered to him if there was or was not. In the past he has come in when the shop has been full and he has started his abusive talk about Jewish people in a loud voice. Today he was as bad as ever. He talked about what had just happened in Germany in many cities and even villages and in parts of Austria where the Nazis and their hired thugs smashed ever window in the shops owned by Jewish businessmen. Klempner said that we Jewish businessmen in St James would have our own night of broken glass. He said he and his friends would be back to night to smash my windows and the windows in Danny Jacobs shop and in Levine and Marcus over the road. I told him to go to hell. When he left the shop I rang at once to the police station and told them about what threats had been made. I asked if they would send a police officer tonight to keep guard. Also I told them about the threat to the other Jewish businesses nearby. The policeman I spoke to, I think he was only a constable who would not connect me to a more senior officer, did not take the matter seriously I thought, although I told him that Klempner would very likely keep his threat as he had on occasions in the past when he had said that he would do things against us.'

Carpenter lowered the diary and looked at Hodgkiss. 'I know it's true what he said about the police. They would do nothing to protect us from these thugs.'

'How old were you when these things were happening?' Hodgkiss asked.

Carpenter raised an eyebrow and Hodgkiss could see him calculating. 'Well, I was born in 1930 so I was eight at the time — just before my eighth birthday in fact.'

'And your father — how old was he at this time?'

'My father would have been around forty. I was three years old when we came here to Australia.'

'And did your family come here to St James as soon as you arrived?'

'You could say so. Some of our friends from Germany were living here already so we came here also to live.'

'And your father bought the house where your son still lives?'

Hodgkiss saw the two other men exchange quick glances.

'My father built that house,' said Carpenter.

'And that's why he doesn't want to sell,' put in Cook.

'I thought that house and your houses, Mr Cook, were all built by some developer who built a whole row of houses in the street. The ones you want to have heritage listed.'

Carpenter shook his head impatiently. 'I said my father built it in the way that people say they build a house when really they arrange for a builder to come and do the job for them. I thought that was a common way of saying this in English.'

'And so it is,' Hodgkiss conceded. 'And how old would you say the Klempners were at that time?'

Carpenter turned to Cook. 'How old would you say they were, Heinrich?'

Cook shrugged. 'Fifty. Maybe a little less, maybe a little more.'

Carpenter nodded. 'Yes. I would have said about fifty. Maybe a little older than my father. Why do you ask, Hodgkiss?'

'I was just trying to form a picture in my mind of the individuals involved in this tragic business.' Hodgkiss pointed to the diary. 'Are you going to tell me what Klempner and his people did? Did he carry out his threat?'

'Did he carry it out? What do you think, Hodgkiss?'

'I know he did, with some help. In fact very recently I read an old newspaper report of acts of vandalism committed in St James at that time.'

'I see you have already done some research, then,' said Carpenter. He hesitated, then continued. 'Hodgkiss, does the word Krystallnacht mean anything to you?'

Hodgkiss nodded. 'Yes. I read about that too. It was the night of November nine-ten German time, was it not?'

Carpenter nodded. 'And you know what happened?'

'Of course.'

'Then I can tell you that something similar happened in St James on the following night, but of course on a much smaller scale. But the same hateful motive was behind it.'

'So there is nothing more to tell," said Cook. 'Now the man knows everything he wants to know.'

Carpenter shook his head. 'Don't be in such a hurry to get rid of him Heinrich. He still doesn't know what happened to the Klempners. How they died.'

'That he doesn't need to know,' said Cook with emphasis.

'But of course he does,' said Carpenter. 'He's a scholar; a man doing research. He wants to know … naturally. Don't you, Hodgkiss?'

'I'd like to know, but not if it's going to make trouble between you and your friend here.'

'How can it make trouble now … for him, for me or for anyone. What can you do? What can anyone do?'

'You tell him if you must,' said Cook. 'But you can tell him by yourself. I don't want to hear that over again.'

Carpenter shrugged. 'Please yourself, Koch. But don't worry; I'm not going into any of the gory details. No one needs that, eh, Hodgkiss?'

'Certainly not,' Hodgkiss said.

'Then what's to tell?' Cook demanded. He turned to Hodgkiss. 'I'll tell you what happened if you must know.'

Hodgkiss held up a hand to stop the words, but it was too late.

'They killed them,' Cook said aggressively. 'Our fathers killed them … the two swine. The night after they smashed the windows in all the shops Oscar's father told them to come to his home. He told them that he would pay them the money they demanded if the Jewish shops were to be left alone and their windows not smashed again as soon as the glass was replaced. As soon as the Klempners came into the house our fathers took them down the hall towards the kitchen at the back. On the way they went into one of the bedrooms where two axes were already hidden behind the door. Oscar's father had told them that we had put the money in a drawer in one of the desks. He said they should stay where they were in the hall. Oscar's father had been careful to put the chain on the front door when they let the Klempners come in so that they could not run out again quickly that way. They attacked them in the hall with the axes and killed them both there. It was too quick and there was not enough pain for them before they died.

'Is that what you wanted to know, Hodgkiss?'

Hodgkiss nodded slowly.

'They had no fear coming into my home,' said Carpenter. 'Such contempt did they have for us that they never dreamed that our fathers would dare to defy them or attack them.

He turned to Cook and nodded towards Hodgkiss. 'He told Michael that he knows what they did with the bodies.'

Cook snorted. 'So he told me too. Well, I don't think so. I think you're all piss and wind, Hodgkiss, to use a good old Aussie saying. Even if you do know — which I doubt — I can't see what good it will do you.'

'No. Nor do I,' said Hodgkiss. 'It can't do me much good. It's certainly not something I'd put in a book even if I every get around to writing one or bothering to check to see if I'm right about it. But it's good to know the truth about things, don't you think. And for that I thank both you gentlemen.'

When Hodgkiss returned to the car the book had fallen from Esme's hand and she was sleeping silently, her head turned to one side, face to the window.

Hodgkiss was about to knock on the glass when he paused, knuckles raised.

She's really quite a lovely girl, he thought. And she hasn't had much of a life so far. No great fun or adventure in it. Not so much as a decent trip overseas. I should pay more attention to her and to what she wants in her life. And Donald too, perhaps. All in all we're a lucky family.

Esme's eyes opened. She smiled at her father.

*   *   *

Esme poured two mugs of tea, black, put two sachets of raw sugar into the pocket of her blouse and carried them through the family room to the back deck.

'Well, Dad,' she said, taking her place opposite her father at the round redwood table. 'Did you find out everything you needed to know for your book?'

She put one of the mugs down in front of her father and placed the two sachets of sugar beside it.

'I'd say I found out *more* than I needed to know. Certainly more than I *wanted* to know.'

'Then it was a case of "too much information," was it?'

Hodgkiss blew across the surface of the tea then nodded. 'Yes. You could say that. Definitely "too much information."'

'So, is it a problem then, what those fellows told you?'

Hodgkiss thought about that. 'I don't know about that. Not a problem really, not now. It all happened so long ago.'

'Then you know what happened to the two fellows who disappeared? What was their name again?'

'Klempner. What happened to them was that they died … murdered.'

'Is that what those fellows told you? That they were murdered. How did they know that?'

'Mr Carpenter's father kept a diary. It was all there, in some detail, although Carpenter did not translate the crucial entry word for word. Mr Cook got in first and put me in the picture, quite graphically too. Their two fathers conspired to do the deed. They killed the two Klempners in Carpenter's home with axes … in the hallway.'

Esme squirmed. 'But that's shocking, Dad. And that's what they told you today; that the two fellows had been murdered, and how their fathers did it.'

'That's all I wanted to know. Of course the circumstances raise quite a number of other questions that I did not feel it was appropriate to ask.'

'Such as?'

'Well, Oscar Carpenter was born in nineteen-thirty, or so he told me and I have no reason to doubt him. That means he would have been about eight when this traumatic event took place in his own home. Probably just outside his bedroom door. I suppose I could have asked him if it was really necessary to consult his father's diary in order to tell me what happened. Surely he would have had personal memories of the event. Just think about it. Young Oscar, age eight, lying in his bed not ten feet from where it happened; from where two men were butchered with axes in the hallway of his family home. Imagine the noise. The shouting, the screaming, the pleading. And think of the blood ... all the blood.'

'I'd much rather not, thank you, Dad. In fact I don't think I want to hear another word about the whole business..

'I suppose it's not beyond the bounds of possibility that young Oscar may have had to assist.'

'Dad!!!! That's enough.'

'Yes. It's enough. But there's still one more thing. The last mystery to be solved.'

'And what's that?'

'Where they buried the Klempner brothers. But that's no great mystery really.'

'No mystery! What, did they tell you that, too?'

Hodgkiss shook his head. 'No. they didn't volunteer to

tell me and I didn't ask. Besides, I know, or I think I know.'

'Why? What makes you think you know that?'

'Because of what you were reading in the *Star* the other day.'

'Do you mean that letter about that ... thing, whatever they call it that the Jewish folk want to put up at St James.'

'The eruv. Yes.'

'But what could that possibly have to do with where they buried those two fellows.'

'The eruv didn't have a great deal to do with it really. But it gave me a clue. It was the reaction of old Oscar Carpenter to the eruv then later to council's plans for the playground that gave their game away. You see, young Michael Carpenter was in favour of the eruv. He made no bones about that. You read his letter in the Star. He said that the Jewish community in St James was so keen on the project that they were even prepared to pay the costs of installing it.

'He even told me that his father was in favour of the eruv until he happened to mention that a pole would have to be installed in the front yard of the family home to help make the connection because all the telegraph lines were on the other side of the street.

'Then his father's attitude changed entirely.'

Esme shook her head. 'But why would that be a problem, just putting up a pole ...' She hesitated. 'Unless ... of course. Oh, yes. Now I see why he might object.'

Hodgkiss nodded. 'Yes. But as if that wasn't bad enough, then along came the council with its plan to buy up all the houses on that side of the street, demolish them and turn the sites into a kiddies' playground.

'That of course would have involved massive upheavals. The homes would have been demolished; the gardens uprooted and even the contours of the land no doubt would have had to be graded because there's quite a slope to the land in that area.

'The estate agent acting for council had already approached both Michael Carpenter and Henry Cook. Of course as soon as the agent had knocked on the door with an offer for his house Cook ran off immediately and told Oscar Carpenter what was in the wind.'

'Which means that Cook must have known about old Mr Carpenter's problem.'

Hodgkiss nodded vigourously. 'Of course he did. Both families must have known. And when I went to visit Carpenter in his nursing home Cook was already there and they were hatching a plan to have that side of the street declared a heritage area which, if it ever happens, will prevent the homes from being demolished and, presumably, stopped any future owner from making dramatic changes to any part of the grounds. It isn't surefire insurance that no one would dig up the lawn or the garden, but it was their best try.'

'So where do you think Mr Carpenter and his neighbour Cook buried them?'

Hodgkiss shrugged. 'Who knows, but the front garden seems the logical place because most of the yard is screened from the street by what looks to me like an old, dense hedge. The back yard slopes away fairly steeply to the houses behind so the yard is overlooked from the rear.'

'So then the extra pole for the eruv would probably have to go in the front yard, wouldn't it?' Esme added.

'Obviously. Nevertheless, I think that Michael could have persuaded his father to go along with the eruv. After all, Oscar could have had the final say about exactly where the pole was to go and make sure that they dug somewhere that wasn't likely to … cause any problems.'

'But aren't you assuming that Michael didn't know what was buried there?'

'Yes. That's very likely indeed, because, according to Michael his father was very reticent about discussing all matters relating to the family history. And Michael could not speak or read German or not very well, or so he told me, so the chances are he never knew about what happened.'

Esme paused, frowning. 'You know, Dad. I find it very hard to believe that Michael didn't know enough German to understand at least some of what was in that diary; that he couldn't read at least a bit of German or find someone to read bits to him.'

'So, you think he knew what was in it, or the parts that matter? So why do you think he gave it to me?'

'Don't you think it's possible that he wanted people to know about what had happened; even to know that the bodies were buried there. Then his father would have no reason left to object to the eruv, if that was the only reason he had for opposing it.'

Hodgkiss, thought about that. 'But he didn't want his father to be able to blame him for the truth coming out. Is that what you had in mind?'

'Well, not that exactly, but it's not a bad explanation, is it. And you coming along doing research on unsolved crimes was a real gift from the gods for Michael, wasn't it?'

Hodgkiss nodded. 'It was indeed. He decided to use me to persuade his father that there was no point in trying to keep the secret of *what*, or rather, *who*, was in the garden. That way *I'd* be responsible for the truth coming out and for any uncomfortable consequences, not him. Yes, Esme. It fits.

His father is well advanced in years and probably quite well off so there is every good reason why young Michael should not do anything even remotely likely to alienate his father's affections.'

'So what are you going to do about it, Dad? Report it to Donald?'

Hodgkiss was aghast. 'Report it to Donald! Whatever for? If there was a crime committed it is so far in the past that …'

'Dad, what do you mean "if?" It … was … murder!'

'Yes, yes, of course it was.' He paused. 'And, on second thoughts, I think you're right, Esme. I will discuss it with Donald when he comes home. After all, I raised the matter with him in the first place. I suppose he's entitled to know the results of my research.'

*　　*　　*

It was just after five o'clock when Hodgkiss, who had been keeping a lookout from his bedroom window at the front of the house, saw Donald turn the unmarked police car into the driveways.

He rose quickly and headed down the hall towards the kitchen. But just as he passed the hall table the cordless phone rang.

He snorted impatiently, but paused and scooped up the handset. 'Yes,' he demanded. 'What is it?'

'You really are a cranky old sod,' came a throaty female voice. 'Sometimes I wonder why on earth I bother to have anything to do with you.'

'It's just that I was about to …'

'Oh there's no need to apologise, Hodgkiss. Not that you were about to.'

'Very well, Jan. I apologise. Now, what can I do for you?'

'What makes you think that *I've* rung *you* for help? Would it never occur to you that someone might ring to offer *you* help? No, I suppose your vanity would never permit it.'

'Well, you're certainly loosing both barrels on me this evening. But I confess I deserved it. So, may we start again? Good evening, Jan. How are you? Well, I trust.'

'Don't overdo it, Hodgkiss. I've only rung to let you know that I've sent you an email that you may find of interest. It has to do with the eruv and the machinations of one of the participants in the battle over the eruv, one M Carpenter. I thought it may give you a new insight into his motives.'

'May I assume that your information does not place him in the kindest of lights?'

'You most certainly may. Now I will release you to attend to what ever pressing task caused your irritation at being sidetracked to take my call.'

'Oh, for heaven's sake, Jan, there's no need to be so touchy, I was only ...' But the line was dead.

Hodgkiss sighed, returned the handset to the phone and headed back to bedroom. He booted up the computer, entered his email and clicked on the latest message.

To <u>ehodgkiss@ozemail.com.au</u>

Just a snippet of information that may prove of interest.

You will recall no doubt that one of the letters in the most recent issue of the Star was signed by one M Carpenter.

Well, one M Carpenter of St James has very recently contacted council's town planning department with an offer to sell his property. This in itself is quite unusual since most citizens — certainly the wise ones — have as little to do with council as possible.

What made the contact additionally interesting was the fact that not only was Carpenter eager to sell but he also made the suggestion that the area in which his family home is located would be extremely suitable for one of the children's playgrounds that council is now, in my view notoriously, proliferating.

He offered all the approved reasons for making the suggestion, in particular the fact that there is a large number of high rise blocks approved in the area thus the playground is needed to cater for the large number of young people who, it is anticipated, will throng these new slums of the future.

The officer in our town planning section who received this correspondence took the trouble to go to our rate books to ascertain whether the ratepayer on this property was in fact M Carpenter and discovered that the owner was one O Carpenter — a close relative no doubt.

The owner before O Carpenter was one K Tischler. I don't suppose you know anything about this gentleman.

Apropos nothing in particular the officer mentioned that there is a view, probably justified in his opinion, that the establishment of an eruv would have a very favourable impact upon property values within the area as homes there would be more enthusiastically sought by adherents of that faith.

Fyifwiw.

JC-J

To jcampbell-jones@canunddacouncil.com.au

Fyi I understand. But fwiw?

EH

To ehodgkiss@ozemail.com.au

For what it's worth!

J-CJ

To <u>jcampbell-jones@kanunddacouncil.com.au</u>

Noted!

And thanks for your email. It contained some very interesting and pertinent information.

The O Carpenter is indeed the owner of the subject property and the M Carpenter, the letter writer, is his son.

You may take it from me that O Carpenter will take a great deal of persuading to sell his property for a park or for any other purpose.

In fact when I spoke to him yesterday both he and his neighbour, Mr Henry Cook, were preparing to make a request to have their properties heritage listed.

Their reasons for seeking this outcome are both extraordinary but, from their point of view, eminently sensible.

Heritage listing of their properties would go a long way towards solving what has become for them a hideous, problem which has plagued them both for more than half a century.

As for the gentleman who owned the property before O Carpenter, that is, K Tischler. It may help you to know that Tischler is German for Carpenter.

The Carpenter's neighbour, Cook, who is also enthu-siastic about heritage listing — a preoccupation which, in itself, must arouse a degree of justifiable suspicion — was previously known as Koch, German for Cook.

Fyihiiu

EH

To <u>ehodgkiss@ozemail.com.au</u>

Hiiu?

To <u>jcampbell-jones@kanunddacouncil.com.au</u>
Hope it is useful!
EH
To <u>ehodgkiss@ozemail.com.au</u>
Noted!

I don't suppose you are going to tell me why you think the reasons which the Carpenters and Cook have for desiring heritage listing are both extraordinary and eminently sensible.
J-CJ

To <u>jcampbell-jones@kanunddacouncil.com.au</u>
Not right now. Be patient.
EH

Hodgkiss closed the email, rose and headed for the kitchen where he could hear Donald in muttered conversation with Esme.

As he approached he heard Esme, say, in exasperated tones: 'Really, Donald, I've no idea. Ask him yourself.'

'Ask me what?' said Hodgkiss pushing open the kitchen door.

Donald rose from the small bar fridge under the kitchen bench, a can of beer in one hand. 'I just want to know what you know about that Carpenter character.'

'Which Carpenter character? There are two of them. Michael Carpenter and his father Oscar.'

'I don't know any Oscar. It's Michael I'm interested in.'

'Why? What's he done?'

'Do you remember me telling you that we'd received word that there had been some unpleasantness over that eruv?'

'Yes, of course I remember, Donald,' Hodgkiss snapped peevishly. 'Do you think I have suffered onset of senile dementia in the past twenty-four hours.'

Donald rolled his eyes, but ploughed on. 'Well, we've had a complaint — an official complaint — about this Michael Carpenter fellah. Bloke called at the police station and reckoned this Michael Carpenter had threatened him unless he cooled his objections to the eruv.'

'And who is this person who made the complaint?'

Donald shook his head. 'Sorry, Dad. Can't tell you that. Anyway, you should know better than to ask.'

'It doesn't matter. It was probably one of those mindless anti-Semitic bigots who've been writing to the paper or one of their cronies in the so-called St James Advancement Society.'

'You're getting warm,' Donald volunteered. 'And Esme told me that she drove you over to the Rosemount nursing home to visit Carpenter's father. Is that right?'

'Of course it's right. Why should Esme tell lies over such a trivial matter?'

'So it was trivial, was it? You didn't learn anything important while you were there, did you? Nothing that might involve the police?'

'And just what did Esme have to say about my visit. She didn't come in with me, you know.'

'Yeah! I know that. She told me she stayed in the car reading. I was just wondering if Carpenter senior told you anything I should know.'

Hodgkiss glanced towards Esme who stood with her back to the stove looking at him anxiously over Donald's shoulder.

She shook her head slowly from side to side.

'No. I don't think so, Donald,' said Hodgkiss. 'Old Oscar Carpenter didn't reveal any hideous secrets that might require immediate police attention. What has his son had to say about the allegations against him?'

Donald shrugged. 'No idea. Uniform division is handling

it. Why do you reckon he'd be making threats like that against people opposing this eruv thing?'

'Greed, Donald. Naked greed. Jan Campbell-Jones told me that there is a view that if the eruv is approved it will do wonders for the value of properties inside the boundary because members of that faith will clamour to buy into the area. Could be true, I suppose. I'd say Carpenter junior is taking pre-emptive action against anyone who might prevent him realizing full value on the property.'

Donald nodded. 'Yeah! I suppose so.' He turned to Esme. 'So what's for dinner?'

*   *   *

It was a week later when Donald arrived home unexpectedly for lunch.

He took a can of beer from the fridge then walked through to the back deck to join Hodgkiss while Esme prepared a plate of sandwiches.

Hodgkiss was sitting, reading, at the redwood table. He looked up from his paperback novel. 'And what brings you home in the middle of the day, Donald? Crime taken a holiday in Kanundda, has it?'

Donald pulled the ring tab from the beer can and took a hearty gulp. 'You could say that. The business I've just been to wasn't actually a crime, I suppose. More of a disturbance I think you'd call it, although the council may decide to take some sort of action over it.'

When Hodgkiss failed to comment Donald raised the beer can again and took another thirsty gulp.

'It's about those two Carpenters; the father and son. You remember; you visited the old man in the nursing home and the son had been reported for making threats about that eruv arrangement?'

'Yes, Donald, Of course I remember. I'm hardly likely to forget,' said Hodgkiss wearily. 'What about them?'

'Well, I was up in East Kylerbrin where there'd been a break-in and I was on my way back to the station when this call came over about a disturbance in the street where that Carpenter fellow lives, so I thought I'd go along and have a look-see. A couple of the neighbours had rung in complaining because there was a bloody big piece of earth-moving equipment at work in the front yard of the Carpenter's place and the neighbours reckoned that there hadn't been approval for any work at that address, and they were right too, because I made a quick check with your friend at the council and she said that there hadn't been even an application let alone approval for a swimming pool or a car port or any kind of building work there.'

Donald paused and glanced across the table anticipating some comment, but Hodgkiss appeared to be absorbed, examining the dial of his wristwatch.

So Donald continued. 'Apparently old Oscar Carpenter and his old mate Cook from next door had taken it into their heads to build a swimming pool in Carpenter's front yard.

'When I got there the two of them were standing around supervising the workmen.'

'I don't suppose you know the name of the company they'd hired to do the work?' Hodgkiss said, apparently interested now in Donald's story.

Donald shook his head. 'Well, they didn't have a sign up giving the name of the builders like you see sometimes where there's work going on, but I've found out since from one of the neighbours that Carpenter hired the bobcat and the men who were doing the work from a construction company run by one of his Jewish mates who happens to live not far away. Apparently the workmen just rocked up there this morning with the bobcat without a by-your-leave and they'd dug up half the yard and carted all the dirt away in two ruddy great trucks before we got there and put a stop to it.'

Hodgkiss stifled a chuckle by turning it into a rasping cough.

Donald ignored this performance. 'When I contacted old man Carpenter and told him that they'd have to stop work immediately and apply for permission through the proper channels he didn't make a fuss. Went quiet as a lamb. It seemed to me that he couldn't have cared less about it any more. Then all the workmen packed up, put the bobcat on the back of a loader and drove off. But I tell you what, he's got one hell of a hole in his front yard now.

'I reckon his son will go ballistic, particularly if he's still planning to sell the place.'

'Who cares what his son thinks,' said Hodgkiss. 'Besides, I've no doubt the place will be sold before much longer. That should make him happy again.'

'Why do you say that, Dad? I thought his father didn't want to sell. Word is that he was all fired up to have it heritage listed so that no one could ever touch it. I guess he'll soon change his mind about that because the whole place looks a terrible mess now and it wouldn't be cheap to tidy it up without a major landscaping operation.'

Donald paused to take another gulp of beer. Then a thought occurred to him.

'Hey! Where d'you think old Oscar and his mates dumped all the dirt they dug out of that ruddy great hole?'

Hodgkiss shrugged and shook his head. 'I shouldn't worry about that if I was you, Donald. It's hardly a police matter, is it … illegal dumping? Besides, they're not likely to tell you anyway.'

'Oh! And why do you say that?'

'Well, they're not about to tell anyone where they dumped it for fear of being prosecuted.'

Donald put his empty can down heavily on the table. He looked across at his father-in-law then lifted a hand, finger raised aggressively as if about to address an angry question.

Hodgkiss look up sharply and met his son-in-law's eye.

Slowly and emphatically Hodgkiss shook his head.

'Ask no questions and you'll be told no lies!'

*   *   *

It was more than two months later. Hodgkiss was sitting in the breakfast nook reading the morning paper.

His attention had been caught by the heading on a short item at the bottom of an inside page.

HIKERS GRISLY FIND IN BUSH

The story read –

Three hikers made an alarming discovery of bones while walking in the Kanundda National Park.

The bones, believed to be human remains, were found at the site of what is believed to be an illegal tip.

Crestwood Police are investigating.

Suddenly Hodgkiss became aware of Donald standing bedside him, reading over his shoulder.

'Don't worry, Dad. It's one helluva mess out there. There's been a torrent of water through the whole area after all that rain we had the week before last. There's no way in the world anyone will ever be able to tell exactly where any of that dirt came from.'

Hodgkiss nodded, relieved, and turned the page.

Hodgkiss and the Empty Room

'**Y**ou'd do well to mind your own business, Sarah, and not waste any sympathy on that adulterous pair.'

Thus did Adrian Whitten admonish his sister, Sarah Rainer, when she raised for the umpteenth time her brother's treatment of a couple who had, in her view, the misfortune to work for him.

Adrian had caught the two, Eric Furlough and Janice Evers, on CCTV having after-hours sex in the office where they worked.

The three people who worked under Adrian in that division of the Kanundda Council, which was housed in an old building distant from the main council chambers, had long believed that the small CCTV system which covered their office was out of service.

But over one recent long weekend Adrian had spent several hours restoring it to use without mentioning this to either Eric, Janice or David Caton, a junior who cheerfully performed any menial task asked of him.

So when Whitten confronted the couple with CCTV vision of what he referred to as their 'horrid betrayal' they had felt both outraged and alarmed.

When asked by Furlough what he intended to do with the innocuous-looking silver disk on which his activities with Janice Evers were recorded, Adrian had merely smiled in his unpleasant way and said that was a matter to which he would have to give serious thought.

Some time later, when Sarah surprised him one evening viewing the disk at home on his personal computer, she too had asked him the same question; what did he intended to do with what he called his 'evidence'.

He had evaded her question and told her she would do well to mind her own business.

'You call it evidence, do you?' she said angrily. 'I call it sneaky spying ... and it's probably against the law.'

'Nonsense,' he snapped. 'There's nothing illegal about CCTV cameras. These days they're everywhere. Why, if it wasn't for CCTV half of the criminals in the Sydney would never be caught. Besides, that pair's behaviour is quite beyond the pale. It's a disgrace.'

'It's nothing of the sort,' Sarah snapped. 'It's just two people making love. It goes on everywhere, Adrian. But of course you wouldn't know anything about that, would you? You've never been in love.'

'Love,' he sneered, looking up from the screen. 'Do you call that love? A man carrying on with a married woman behind her husband's back. Lust. That's what I call it. It has nothing to do with love.'

'Really,' snapped Sarah. 'And what makes you such an authority on love.'

Adrian gave his sister an unpleasant, humourless smile. He shook his head. 'Nothing. There I must bow to your superior experience. You've certainly had enough practice in the love-making department. Even poor Clive eventually woke up to your adulterous ways and cleared out.'

This reference to Sarah's ex-husband did nothing to lighten the atmosphere. 'He was a dry old stick, was Clive,' she said. 'And kindly leave him out of this if you don't mind. What I do with my life is my business.'

'Is that what you think is it? Well I'd say it becomes *my* business too, particularly when you bring a parade of drunken boyfriends home here for the night. You seem to have forgotten that you live here only by my good grace and I can tell you my patience is wearing pretty thin, particularly after Friday night. Don't you ever bring that drunken lout into my home again.'

Sarah retreated to the kitchen where she turned her attention to the hotplate. She thought: Yes, bringing Charles home was a mistake. And there was no need. We could just as easily have managed it in his car.

And her brother's reference to his 'good grace' was a reminder of the threat that hung constantly over her.

Contrary to the family solicitor's advice, their ageing parents, always careful with money, had written a will in which their parsimonious son was given control over the considerable funds left in trust for their wayward daughter.

Their low opinion of Sarah was confirmed when her marriage broke down shortly before they died within a few weeks of each other.

When Sarah's husband left her after discovering that she had been indulging in serial affairs, he had arranged his finances so that in the wash-up from the divorce Sarah found herself penniless.

Thus she was flung back, unwillingly, upon her brother's offer of a home.

Adrian had been quick to take advantage of the situation and quickly reduced his sister to the role of housekeeper/cook, forced to survive on a tiny allowance.

'I wonder those two have stuck it out with you at the Unit for as long as they have,' Sarah said when Adrian appeared in the kitchen. 'Working for you would be no picnic.'

Adrian took his place at the breakfast bar. 'They stay because they'd never get the same money working anywhere else. Computer programmers like Janice Evers are twenty to the dozen these days, and he's just a glorified electrician. There's a hundred applicants for every job of the sort that he does. They're on a good wicket working in what's left of our Unit and they know it.'

'Financially maybe,' Sarah conceded. 'But they'd need to be well paid to put up with you, Adrian.'

She cracked an egg into an iron pan already spitting with olive oil and butter. 'You know, Adrian, it's a wonder that poor Eric fellow hasn't taken to you with an axe before now.'

*   *   *

'I find it near impossible to believe that there is not a single tasty scandal worth reporting about any one of those spineless apologies for a human being who you have the misfortune to manage.'

Edgar Hodgkiss was sitting at one of the tiny round tables in the forecourt of Frendz Coffee Shop in West Lillimoor. Opposite him, with her knees touching, sat the General Manager of Kanundda Council, Jan Campbell-Jones.

Hodgkiss and Jan met at irregularly intervals at Frendz

often to discuss and attempt to solve the numerous problems which plagued the administration of the council. Several times they had, between them, devised stratagems to avoid or at least ameliorate the worst consequences of disastrous decisions made by the council's corrupt majority faction.

Jan shook her head. 'Hodgkiss, I'm sorry to disappoint you. I promise if there was any scandal worthy of the name concerning any of my councillors, even of the most trivial nature, I would not hesitate to regale you with the details. But the truth is that at the moment, believe it or not, there is absolutely nothing naughty to report.

'However, one scrap of juicy gossip comes to mind, but it does not involve an elected member of council … merely staff.'

Hodgkiss leaned forward. 'Beggars can't be choosers. Actually I often find scandals involving ordinary every-day people far more interesting than the doings of so-called celebrities.'

'Then you should find this to your taste because those involved could certainly be classified as "ordinary every-day people." Have you ever heard of our Specialist IT Unit?'

Hodgkiss shook his head. 'No. What do they do there?'

'It's really more a matter of what they *used* to do. When we began installing computers throughout our offices we needed people who were experts in the field; people who could install the hardware, put on the various programmes we were using, then help out when our people started having problems which, as you could imagine, was very often, at first.

'So in those early days the IT Unit was a pretty sizeable and busy operation.

'But then as our staff became more conversant with the things and worked out how to solve problems for themselves, the demand for a centralized pool of expertise fell away to the point where now there's only four people in the Unit and you can take it from me that they're not exactly overworked these days.

'They operate out of a small office building not far from here actually. I've been meaning to close them down and bring the staff, all four of them, back to head office and find them some proper work to do. I've already told them so and no one really minds except of course the fellow in charge, a fellow who enjoys playing the tyrant in his tiny realm.'

Hodgkiss asked: 'And this is where the juicy home-grown scandal has occurred? I suppose with such a small staff it's probably just a case of propinquity overwhelming good sense.'

Jan nodded. 'I'd say that's about the size of it. First allow me to introduce you to the cast of this little drama. The villain of the piece is Adrian Whitten, head of the unit, a misanthrope of about sixty years who lives with a younger sister whom he holds in a form of slavery since her husband managed to conceal all of the family assets before he divorced her, having discovered her multiple affairs. Now the poor woman is forced to dance attendance on her horrid brother for very little reward, or so the stories go.

'Next there are our two star-crossed lovers: Eric Furlough and Janice Evers. Janice is a comely young woman who, unfortunately for her, already has a husband who may or may not be aware of his wife's lapse from conjugal fidelity.

'Eric Furlough is not my idea of the leading man in a romantic drama. He is tall, dark, but not particularly handsome although he has the advantage of being single.

'Then there is the light relief played by a young fellow by the name of David Caton. David is the general dogsbody in the office; he runs messages, takes phone calls, leaves 'while you were out' notes for the others when they go on long lunches etc.

'Young David lives an idyllic working life with no particularly onerous duties or responsibilities. Of course years ago, when the Unit was in full swing, he was run off his little feet taking calls for help, following them up to make sure the jobs were done and taking all the abuse when they weren't.'

Hodgkiss asked. 'And would I be correct in assuming that it is this Mercury who is your messenger, your source of information about this little drama?'

'Now that's very perceptive of you, Hodgkiss. What made you think of that?'

'Well, who else but the carefree foot-loose dogsbody could be your source, since the other three were intimately involved in the drama, thus unlikely to talk about it.'

Jan tossed her head slightly to the left. 'And speak of the devil. Here comes my young Mercury, and from here I'd say he looks like someone with some interesting gossip who can scarcely contain himself.'

Hodgkiss turned to see a young man of about twenty, tall with unruly brown hair, approaching, threading his way dexterously through the maze of small tables set out in the courtyard. There was no mistaking his air of puppy-like eagerness.

Jan made the introductions. 'Edgar Hodgkiss, this is David Caton. David works at our Special IT Unit.'

David thrust out a hand. 'Great to meet you Mr Hodgkiss. Love your letters. Keep 'em coming.'

This was a reference to the flow of letters which Hodgkiss wrote to the editor of the local free newspaper, *The Northern Star,* letters usually critical of some aspect of the operations of the Kanundda Council. Many of these relied on information provided anonymously to Hodgkiss by disgruntled members of the council's staff who viewed with disgust the scams which councillors worked from time to time to enrich themselves at the expense of the ratepayers.

'Sit yourself down, David,' said Jan. 'Am I right in assuming you have dropped by to bring us up to date on the latest state of affairs at the Uni?.'

David pulled out one of the small wrought iron chairs and sat down. He leaned forward conspiratorially.

'You'll never guess what Whitten's done now. He's posted them on the internet.'

Jan shook her head in disgust. 'What! Photos of Janice and Eric?'

David nodded eagerly. 'Yes. But he blanked out their faces.'

'And were they actually …?'

'At it, d'you mean? Yes. Not a stitch on and anyone who knows our office could tell where the picture was taken because they were doing it on her desk and you could see the photocopier and coffee machine in the background.'

'Well, luckily very few people would be able to identify them from their surroundings,' said Jan, 'since no one, or hardly anyone, visits that place any more.'

David nodded. 'True enough, but I suppose her husband might recognise her even with her face blanked out.'

'Yes, I suppose he might. Does he ever call in at the unit, do you know?'

David shook his head. 'No. I don't remember ever seeing him there.'

'Then she might get away with it. But it makes you wonder why Whitten bothered doing it.'

'Knowing him I'd say he did it just to torment them. He's a really weird person.'

'In what other ways is he weird?' Hodgkiss asked.

'He never comes out to our office. He keeps the door between his office and our area permanently locked and bolted on his side. If he wants to tell us anything he rings on one of the internal phones or comes and talks to us through the door.

'In fact I don't think any of us has been in his office for weeks … or longer. Now if that isn't weird I don't know what is.'

He paused, lowered his voice and continued. 'And there's another thing. You know how the four of us put in for a lottery ticket each draw?'

Jan shook her head. 'No. I didn't know that. How long's that been going on?'

'Oh for years. Ever since the Unit was established. In the early days when we had more people sometimes we'd buy three lottery tickets each time. Of course now, with just the four of us there, we buy one ticket. And guess what … we won.'

'Congratulations,' said Jan. 'How much?'

'It wasn't the first prize of course or everyone would know about it by now. But it was a good prize. Really worth winning. Just over eight thousand dollars.'

'Well that must have made everyone happy.'

'You'd think so, wouldn't you, but nothing of the sort. Bloody Whitten isn't paying us our shares.'

'What!' Hodgkiss exploded. 'How can he get away with that?'

David shrugged. 'At first he didn't even tell us about it. Then when he didn't say anything Janice got suspicious and checked on our ticket number and tackled him about it.'

Hodgkiss asked: 'I take it that this Whitten fellow purchased and held the tickets, is that so?'

'Yes, that's right. The drill was he'd buy a ticket then pin it up on our noticeboard and when that one didn't win anything he'd buy another ticket, take down the old one and put up the new one.'

Hodgkiss nodded. 'I see. Then I assume that Ms Evers must have remembered the number of the winning ticket.'

David nodded. 'Actually some time ago she started making a note of the numbers of our tickets. You see, none of us trusted Whitten … not since he'd started making life difficult for everyone. So Janice would write down our numbers as soon as he put the ticket up on the noticeboard.'

'It can't have been very pleasant working in an atmosphere like that.'

Jan asked: 'And what did Whitten say when Janice confronted him about the winning ticket?'

'He said he'd pay out as soon as they liked but if they insisted on it then the next picture he posted on the internet of Janice and Eric having sex wouldn't have their faces blanked out.'

'Dreadful man,' said Hodgkiss. 'And what about you, David? Why hasn't he paid you? He isn't holding anything nasty over your head too, is he?'

David replied indignantly. 'No, of course not. He's got nothing on me.'

'Then why don't you take a stand and demand your money? I take it there is proof that you've all been making your contributions towards these tickets.'

'Oh yes. Janice keeps a book and makes a note every time we put our money in. Old Whitten couldn't deny we've been making our payments.'

'Then there's nothing to stop *you* from demanding *your* share of the winnings, is there?'

'No, I suppose not. But I don't want to make a fuss because he might make things more difficult for Janice and Eric.'

'Does Janice's husband know about what she's getting up to at work?'

David shrugged. 'No. I guess not. But I wouldn't know really.'

'And does he know about this lottery win that she's supposed to share in?'

'I couldn't say, Mr Hodgkiss. Possibly not.'

But in this David was mistaken.

*   *   *

Rolf Evers had known for some months about his wife's affair with the tall, dark-haired man she worked with. When it came to his attention through a phone call from a workmate in the parks and gardens division of the Kanundda Council, Rolf had been upset, but not surprised.

They had been married for twelve years. Rolf, a short man, running to fat even in his teens and with a distinct cast in one eye which grew more noticeable with the passing years, had always experienced problems in attracting the opposite sex. So he had been surprised when Janice, who he thought of as a 'dish', had agreed to his proposal of marriage after a short courtship. Now in her mid-thirties he knew that she was still attractive to men, and he could not deny that their marriage had deteriorated into a boring, loveless routine.

He understood that any attempt to reproach Janice for her misconduct would be totally hypocritical since he, too, had indulged in a number of brief and rather unsatisfactory affairs in recent years.

But for his wife to be robbed of substantial winnings in

a lottery … well, that was a different matter altogether. That demanded solidarity and action.

Information about the win and Whitten's refusal to pay-out had come to Rolf's ears via the same friend as the news of his wife's affair.

He had considered various ways in which he could apply pressure on Whitten to 'do the right thing' as he referred to the situation in discussions with the friend. But as yet he had decided upon no definite course of action.

He had consulted an acquaintance with a law degree who worked in the Kanundda Council's legal department, but the news there was not encouraging. Physical possession of the winning ticket, he was told, was essential to a successful legal action.

He had asked his wife if she knew where Whitten kept the ticket but she could tell him only that it had been taken down from the notice board immediately after the lottery was drawn and removed from the office. As yet no new ticket had been pinned up in its place since the three members of the syndicate who had not received their winnings had refused to continue paying.

On three occasions Rolf had driven to the Unit's rather run-down office block, parked his car in a side-street and taken a window seat in a coffee shop directly opposite the Unit. From there he had kept surveillance on the movements of the staff with particular attention to Whitten's habits.

He knew from a description that Janice had once given of the internal layout that Whitten's office was at the front of the building. It had a side door that opened onto a driveway that led to the rear of the site. The office, where the others worked, he knew, made up the rear of the building.

On one occasion Rolf had arrived at his post in the coffee

shop shortly before five. He had been there only three min-utes before Furlough appeared in the parking area at the rear of the building, chatting with David Caton. The two had walked to a small sports car and with Furlough behind the wheel the car drove slowly up the driveway, paused at the footpath then turned into the street and disappeared in the direction of the highway.

Minutes later Janice left the building and walked quickly out of sight in the direction of the small car park behind the offices. Moments later she appeared edging cautiously up the driveway before she too turned into the street and accelerated away towards the highway.

Whitten did not appear for at least another half an hour. It was almost dark before he emerged through the side door in his office directly onto the driveway. He walked away towards the rear of the building and shortly afterwards drove away in his expensive, late model sedan.

Rolf did not follow because he knew where Whitten lived; an old-fashioned but comfortable-looking block of flats near the railway station at Kylerbrin. He had followed him home on two earlier occasions. Once he had seen a woman standing at the entry door to the flats. Apparently the woman had been waiting for him and the two had engaged in what appeared to Rolf to be a flaming argument before entering the build-ing together.

Two days later Rolf was again at this post in the coffee shop. This time, because he had arrived a little later than usual, he had not bothered to park his car at a distance, but instead had parked it in a vacant spot directly outside.

He skimmed through a newspaper which an earlier cus-tomer had left on a nearby table, looking up from time to time to check for any movement opposite.

Once he looked up in time to see a young man, who from his sister's infrequent comments on life at the Unit, he took to be David Caton, walking up the driveway.

The young man paused near the top of the driveway then turned and disappeared through the doorway in the side wall near the front of the building where he had seen Whitten emerge.

When nothing more happened Rolf picked up the newspaper and resumed reading.

Minutes later he caught a movement out of the corner of his eye and looked up in time to see a woman crossing the road directly towards his car. She appeared to be quite unsteady on her feet. She paused briefly in the middle of the road, swaying slightly as she fumbled in her bag and drew out a remote. Rolf saw her raise an arm, pointing the remote towards his car.

She paused for a moment, baffled when the lights flashed on and off on a car parked directly in front of his. This car, he noted, was identical with his own.

The woman altered course to the other car, opened the driver's door, climbed in and was gone in a moment.

He thought he knew the woman; Sarah Rainer, Whitten' sister, who he had met once or twice at functions at the unit in its happier, more sociable days.

He glanced at his watch; 4:45. He sipped his coffee and resumed his perusal of the newspaper.

When he looked up again shortly afterwards he saw David Caton halfway up the driveway walking quickly towards the road.

Rolf was puzzled. Finally he decided that David must have forgotten something and gone back to fetch it; possibly money or a shopping list.

He was now walking briskly away in the direction of the shops.

Shortly afterwards the waitress delivered Rolf another cup of coffee. A sexy little piece, he thought. It might be worth the effort of chatting her up and see if it was likely to lead to anything. He watched her with more than passing interest as she wiggled her way back to the kitchen.

Rolf glanced again at his watch: 4:53.

He was just about to pay his bill and leave when he saw the side door of the Unit building open. Whitten stepped out, closed the door and stood in the driveway, looking about uncertainly.

Hastily Rolf placed a note on his table, rose and almost ran to the door.

An opportunity like this may not come again.

He hurried into the street, looked both ways for traffic, and crossed the road.

Whitten was still standing in the driveway, frowning, looking about uncertainly, mumbling to himself. As Rolf approached Whitten turned and began to walk unsteadily towards the rear of the building.

As he drew near Rolf was alarmed to see Whitten was holding in his right hand what looked like a gun.

*   *   *

Detective Inspector Donald Burke glanced at the time on his mobile phone. 4.58.

He sighed, rose and crossed to the room's only window. It had been a frustrating kind of day. A series of meetings to discuss various aspects of that latest social fad, community policing. Donald had long held the view that all the community expected of its police was that they turn up promptly when required to assist and to keep serious offenders out of the way of the law-abiding majority.

It had been a day when there had been absolutely no proper police work done, that is, investigating crime and catching criminals.

He was about to clear his desk and go home when his phone rang.

'Inspector Burke,' he said.

The voice at the other end, a woman's, spoke rapidly, frantically.

'Can someone please come quickly? I think our boss may have shot himself.'

'And you are…? Donald inquired politely.

'My name is Janice Evers. But can you please hurry. He may be still alive and we might be able to help him.'

'And who is this person who you think might have shot themselves?'

'His name's Adrian Whitten. He's the head of the office where I work.'

'And you work for this Mr Whitten.'

'Yes. I've just said so.'

'And why do you think he's shot himself.'

'Because we heard what sounded like a gun shot coming from his room and we can't get him to answer the door … and it's locked.'

'Isn't there another key you can use to open it?'

'No. Not that I know of. But Adrian's key is still in the lock anyway so it wouldn't be any good even if we had another key.'

'Then is there a window where you can look in to see what's happened?'

'Yes, there's a window but the curtain's pulled across and

we can't see in. Can you please hurry?'

'Where are you calling from?'

'From our office, at the Kanundda Council's IT unit in West Lillimoor.'

Donald nodded. 'I know the place. I'll be there shortly.'

It was 5.15 when Donald stopped his unmarked police car outside the council's IT Unit where two people, a woman and a man, were waiting anxiously side by side on the kerbside as he pulled up.

As he approached the woman stepped forward. Donald asked: 'I take it you are Mrs Evers, the lady who rang?'

Janice nodded and introduced the man as Eric Furlough.

Donald asked. 'Now, where's this room where you heard a shot?'

'Follow me please, Inspector,' said Janice leading the way quickly down the driveway beside a square brick building.

As they passed the side of the building Donald noticed a wooden door with a Yale-style lock set into the side wall near the front of the building.

Janice noticed and explained: 'That door leads into Mr Whitten's room. That's where the shot came from, in there, but you can't get in through that door because he always keeps it locked and bolted. Besides we haven't got a key.'

'And this is the only window to his room,' Janice continued, indicating a window as they hurried by. 'But as you see he's got the curtain drawn and it'd be locked too. His room's always locked up whether he's in there or not. Security, he says.'

They continued down the side of the building until they reached a large yard at the rear where three cars were parked in neatly marked bays. In the rear wall of the building was a single door. Janice pulled the door open. 'In here,' she said.

Donald followed her into a spacious office with modern workstations built around three of the walls. Only three of these appeared to be in use.

'That's the door to Mr Whitten's room,' said Janice indicating a door in the far wall.

Donald approached the door and dropped to one knee. A key blocked the old-fashioned mortise lock. He knocked loudly on one of the panels in the wooden door.

When there was no response he turned to the others. 'I suppose we'd better have a look inside. You're quite sure that he's in there? He didn't go home early?'

Eric Furlough shook his head. 'No. He's always the last person to leave. He's made a practice of it. Besides, his car's still out back in the parking area.'

Donald sighed. 'I see. OK then, we'd better get this door down, hadn't we, and see what's happened to your Mr Whitten.'

The door offered little resistance to Donald's bulk and flew open at the second shoulder charge.

He stumbled awkwardly into the room, the other two close on his heels.

Donald looked about. A massive desk littered with paper work stood against the far wall. Beside it and set at right angles was a smaller desk on which stood a computer and a clutter of other equipment. The biggest TV set Donald had ever seen hung on the right hand wall.

'Well, your boss certainly isn't here so he must have managed to get out somehow.'

He hurried across to the door in the left hand wall near the front of the room where a strong slightly rusty bolt was closed firmly in the door jamb.

'Well he certainly didn't go out that way.'

As he was about to return to the outer office Donald noticed that the door he had forced open also had a large bolt fitted to the inside and the bolt had ripped a section of wood out of the door jamb.

'Did your boss always lock and bolt himself in like this?' Donald asked indicating the shattered wood of the door jamb.

Furlough nodded. 'Yes, he's very security conscious,' said Furlough.

'And does anyone else work here apart from you two and Mr Whitten?'

'Yes, there's a young fellow by the name of David Caton. He's out at the shops at the moment.'

'And was he here when you heard this shot?'

Janice thought for a moment. 'No. I think he'd just gone out but he may have heard something from the street. He should be back any minute and you can ask him.'

Donald returned to the desk and began a search of the drawers. When nothing of interest caught his attention he turned to the computer.

Minutes later he looked up to see a young man standing near the door to the outer office.

'David Caton, is it?'

'Yes, officer,' said David. 'I've just heard about Mr Whitten. That's really odd. I wonder where he's got to.'

'Yes, meanwhile would you join the others in the other office. I'll be there shortly. I'll want a statement from each of you. Did you happen to hear a gunshot at all after you'd left to go to the shops?'

David shook his head. 'No. I didn't hear anything like that.'

Later, when he had taken statements from the three staff members, he asked: 'You don't think this shot you heard could have been a car backfiring in the street do you?'

Janice shrugged. 'I suppose it may have been,' she conceded. 'Personally I probably wouldn't know the difference between a car backfiring and a gun shot.'

The other two nodded agreement.

Donald thought: well, they're not going to be a lot of help.

As they were leaving the scene-of-crime officers arrived.

'It's not quite the drama we first thought,' he said apologetically. 'Bit of a mystery how the fellow got out of his office with both the doors bolted and the window locked.

'I suppose you'd better have a quick look around and see if anything jumps out at you, but there's no need to spend a lot of time on it.'

*   *   *

Next morning, seated at the built-in pine breakfast nook in the kitchen of his Lillimoor home, Donald Burke looked across the narrow table at his father-in-law.

'Hey Dad,' he said. 'I've got another locked room mystery for you if you're interested.'

Edgar Hodgkiss looked up from his breakfast of two soft-boiled eggs and toast. 'Indeed. And might one be given the particulars of this mystery?'

'I don't see why one might not,' said Donald grandly, 'particularly since no crime was committed.'

'A locked room mystery and no crime committed; a novelty indeed,' said Hodgkiss, scooping white from one of the eggs. 'And why do you say there was no crime committed?'

'Because there was no dead body in the locked room. Sorry to disappoint you, Dad.'

'I am not in the least bit disappointed, Donald. Locked

room mysteries always intrigue me whether there is a body or not.'

'I suppose if there's a mystery at all it's because there *wasn't* a body there.

'Two of the people who work there reckon they heard a gunshot coming from the room.

'But when I got there and finally had to brake the door down the room was empty.

'So somehow the last person in that room, the boss of the unit, managed to walk out and leave it sealed up tighter than a drum.'

'Well that's a promising start for a mystery,' said Hodgkiss. 'Now where is this mysterious locked room to be found?'

'It's in West Lillimoor. Not far from that coffee shop where you sometimes meet Jan to chew the fat. In fact the place where it happened is a part of the Kanundda Council. It's known as the IT Unit.'

With an effort Hodgkiss concealed his surprise. He debated briefly whether or not to inform Donald of the conversation he had with Jan and what he had learned from David Caton about the tense situation at the Unit, but decided, for the present, to remain silent.

'And who are the people involved in this mysterious little drama?'

'Well, there's not many of them that work at this place … only four in fact. First of all there's the fellow who works in the locked room who's apparently gone missing after a shot was supposedly heard coming from his room.'

'Supposedly?'

'Well, the two who heard the shot admitted that they wouldn't know the different between a gun shot and a car backfiring.'

'And the name of the man who is apparently missing is …?'

'Adrian Whitten. The other people who work at this Unit are a man and woman; Eric Furlough and Janice Evers, and a young fellow by the name of David Caton.'

Hodgkiss nodded. 'And are they all agreed about hearing this shot?'

'Ms Evers and Furlough heard it, but young Caton wasn't there at the time.'

'Where was he?'

'Out shopping, according to what they said.'

'"According to what they said"? What does that mean, Donald? Was he out shopping or was he not?'

'Yes, he was,' said Donald tersely. 'What does it matter if he was out shopping or taking a stroll for the good of his health? He wasn't there at the time.'

'And do you know whose shopping he was doing? Had he gone shopping for himself or had one of the others asked him to go to the shops?'

'I've no idea whose idea the shopping was and I don't see that it matters,' Donald snapped. 'Why are you trying to make such a big deal out of this?'

'Really, Donald, you lack the even the smallest crumb of imagination or curiosity. Here we have a man who has apparently vanished from his room in most mysterious circumstances. Two of his workmates claim to have heard a gun shot in his room after which they must have tried to attract his attention without success.

'In those circumstances when you broke open the door you must have expected to find someone in the room since there was apparently no way in or out. You may also have expected to find an occupant suffering from a bullet wound, probably self-inflicted.

'Furthermore, one of the three people who normally would have been a witness to this extraordinary sequence of events just happened to be absent from the building at the crucial time and yet you seem to be not at all concerned to establish the reason for his absence or who was responsible for him being absent. Didn't it cross your mind that he may have been directed to leave the building on some pretext so that he would not be a witness to what took place?'

'OK. OK. I get the picture. So what do you think happened?'

'Really, Donald. I have no idea, but it is something I intend to find out.'

Donald sighed. 'You know what, Dad. I'm sorry I even mentioned this business to you. Can we just drop the whole thing?'

Hodgkiss shrugged. 'As you wish, Donald. But I am confident that you have not heard the last of events at this IT Unit.'

Hodgkiss slid out of the breakfast nook and headed quickly for his bedroom at the front of the house. There he booted up his computer and went to his email.

Firstly, he checked that there was nothing in his Inbox requiring immediate attention then he began typing.

Email to <u>jcampbell-jones@Kanunddacouncil.com.au</u>

It appears that events at your IT Unit have come to a head far sooner and far more dramatically than we thought. In case you have not heard there was a series of dramatic events there yesterday afternoon which I will outline for you.

Donald attended the Unit yesterday afternoon after receiving a phone call from Janice Evers.

During the course of this call Ms Evers told Donald

that she and her colleague, Eric Furlough, had heard what they took to be a gun shot apparently originating from Whitten's office. They beat on his door to attract his attention but there was no response from within. His room, as usual, was locked.

When they became seriously concerned they rang the police and Donald responded. In true Donald Burke fashion, finding the door locked, he forced entry only to discover that the room was unoccupied.

Now this is the interesting bit; not only was the room unoccupied but it was entirely sealed. The door which Donald broke down was locked with the key in the lock on the inside of the door and it was also bolted in the best tradition of locked room mysteries.

A second door, opening to a driveway at the side of the building, was secured with a Yale lock and it was also bolted with what Donald described as a large slightly rusty bolt.

A curtain was drawn over the room's only window which was also secured with the traditional butterfly fastener.

So there we have the basis for a classic locked room murder but without the body.

So far as Donald is concerned there is nothing further to be done. No doubt in due course Whitten will reappear either in the land of the living or, more probably elsewhere. Elsewhere, I fancy.

Meanwhile I think it would be appropriate for you and I to make an inspection of this fascinating location. Tomorrow being Saturday I assume the IT Unit will be deserted and we will be free to conduct a preliminary inquiry.

One aspect of the matter which intrigues me is the fact

that David Caton was absent from the building when this shot was heard. He had gone to shops nearby just before the shot and returned while Donald was conducting his inquiries. I am interested to know who suggested that he should go shopping during office hours. Could you find this out for me as I think it may be of some importance; a view not shared by Donald.

EH

Email to ehodgkiss@ozemail.com.au

I will make the inquiry about David Caton's shopping excursion and I will pick you up from your home at nine in the morning. I share your curiosity about this event.

JC-J

*   *   *

Next morning Hodgkiss was waiting on the nature strip outside the Burke's home when Jan pulled her council-owned sedan over to the kerb on the dot of nine.

When Hodgkiss had fastened his seat belt Jan lean across and kissed him firmly on the lips.

'I had anticipated a rather boring weekend dominated by shopping and housework,' said Jan. 'Now this little escapade of yours has made my day. Tell me, Hodgkiss. What do you expect to learn from our visit to the Unit?'

'Really, Jan. I've no idea. This inspection is purely speculative.'

Jan smiled. 'I don't believe it. I know you well enough to realise that already you've got some idea forming in that devious brain of yours, particularly since there's a mysterious locked room involved in the equation.'

Hodgkiss nodded. 'Yes, the locked room element certainly elevates our quest from the mundane to a higher and more challenging level.'

Jan said. 'I have an answer to your question about young Caton's trip to the shops. Janice gave him some money to go to the corner shop to buy milk for their coffee. That's what she told me. He went off happy as Larry to do her bidding.'

'Was that usual or was it a one-off request?'

'I gather that he frequently did messages of that kind for both of them and sometimes for Whitten. He said they'd not been very busy at the Unit and he was delighted to have the chance to get outside the four walls. Is that what you expected?'

Hodgkiss nodded. 'I fear it is exactly what I expected.'

'Then the shopping trip was a diversion to get him out of the office while Janice and Eric did … whatever it was they did. Is that your idea?'

'Yes, and our challenge is to establish what that was … what did they get up to once David had been dispatched to the shops. I assume we'll have no trouble gaining entry to the Unit building.'

'No. Jenny Cope, my P.A., had duplicate keys although whether or not they'll open all the doors remains to be seen.'

Jan turned the car in at the Unit's entry and drove to the parking area at the rear. She climbed out and took a small bunch of keys from her handbag.

Together, Jan and Hodgkiss climbed a short flight of concrete steps to a solid wooden door in the rear wall of the building. Jan sorted quickly through the keys then selected one. She slid it into the lock and pushed the door open.

Before entering the building she turned to Hodgkiss: 'I assume Donald would have no objection to us being here. I mean, it's not a crime scene or anything like that, is it?'

Hodgkiss shook his head emphatically. 'Certainly not, although who's to say that it won't become one in the near future. And as to whether or not Donald would object to us being here, I would predict with one hundred percent certainty that he would have the strongest possible objection, but only because he would certainly persist doggedly in the view that there is nothing to be gained from investigating the quite extraordinary events that occurred here yesterday.'

The two stood side by side, looking about the room.

'OK, Hodgkiss. We're here. Now, where do you want to start?'

'I think we should have a quick look-see in their drawers before we start in Whitten's office,' said Hodgkiss, pulling open the top drawer of the desk at the nearest workstation.

He sorted quickly through all the drawers then moved on to the next workstation.

Rather unwillingly Jan followed suit.

Minutes later Hodgkiss announced, holding up an orange-covered exercise book: 'This appears to have been where Janice Evers made a note of the payments for their lottery tickets and more recently the numbers of the tickets.'

Hodgkiss took a tiny notepad and pencil from his shirt pocket. 'I think it would be advisable to make a note of the number of their winning ticket which I assume is the last number recorded in Janice's book.'

He wrote carefully on the tiny page then returned the exercise book to the desk drawer.

'And what do you make of this,' said Jan holding up a small rectangular plastic pad with a toggle switch in the centre. 'It looks a bit like one of those remotes used to open and close garage doors.'

'Yes, you could be right. We should make further inquiries about that next week when they're back at work.'

Their search of the office drawers revealed nothing further of interest.

'Time to tackle Whitten's office,' said Hodgkiss, nodding his head towards the only door in the far wall. 'That would be his office in there according to Donald description of the building.'

The door stood open and together they entered the room cautiously.

Against the far wall stood an imposing desk with a side table, but the most striking feature of the room was the huge TV set on the right-hand wall. Hodgkiss noted that it was plugged into what appeared to be a new double power point in white plastic, stark against the dark wood of the skirting board.

First Hodgkiss examined the damage to the door jamb where the large stainless steel bolt screwed to the back of the door had torn free. Then he made a thorough scrutiny of the carpet, an expensive Persian rug with an intricate and colourful pattern.

Next he crossed to the external door in the lefthand wall where he examined the bolt on the inside of the door, being careful not to touch it.

'Well,' asked Jan. 'Might one ask what deductions the Oracle of Lillimoor makes from his observations?'

'Don't you start that Oracle of Lillimoor business, thank you, Jan. And as to my deductions, they are simple enough. There are what will very likely prove to be bloodstains on the Persian rug there, there and there,' Hodgkiss said, indicating different spots with the toe of a shoe. 'No doubt Donald did not see them because, unlike me, he was not looking for them and also because they were difficult to detect due to the complex pattern in the rug. There is also what appears to be blood on the handle of that bolt on the external door although Donald may well have mistaken it for rust which is also to be found there, something which I find rather surprising.'

'Really! And why are you surprised to find rust on an old bolt. It looks sturdy enough to me to do the job.'

Hodgkiss shook his head. 'I am not questioning its sturdiness or utility. I am surprised that the bolt is of iron rather than of steel which is the metal usually used in such fixtures, as in the case of the bolt on the door to the general office.'

Jan rolled her eyes. 'Anything else?'

'Yes. Next I wish to inspect the area of the driveway immediately outside this door. Do you have a key?'

Jan examined her bunch of keys. 'Yes, I think this one will do the trick,' she said, holding up a key. 'But you'll have to slide back the bolt.'

Hodgkiss shook his head. 'I think not. I would prefer to leave that bolt untouched for purely forensic reasons. We can walk around and inspect the driveway.'

Hodgkiss walked back through the office, around the side of the building, Jan close behind him. Together, with heads lowered, they scrutinised the concrete of the drive's surface.

'I'd say that might be blood there,' said Jan. 'What do you think, Edgar?'

Hodgkiss looked where Jan was indicating with her toe. He nodded. 'Yes, I'd say you're right. It should be covered to preserve it for examination.'

'That shouldn't be too difficult,' said Jan. 'There's a good-sized metal tray in the kitchen off the main office. That would cover it. I'll go and get it.'

As soon as Jan had disappeared back into the building Hodgkiss heard a phone in Whitten's office start to ring.

He hurried back into the building, through the rear office and into Whitten's office.

He picked up the handset. 'IT Unit,' he announced.

'Who on earth is that?' a female voice inquired. 'I want to speak to Adrian Whitten. Is this his office or do I have the wrong number.'

'No madam,' said Hodgkiss. 'This is Mr Whitten's office. Who is calling please?'

'This is his sister, Sarah Rainer.'

'And how may I help you, Ms Rainer?' Hodgkiss asked politely.

'He's not there then, I take it?'

'No. Not at the moment. May I take a message?'

'Would you just ask him to ring home if and when he turns up?'

'Did he come home last night?' Hodgkiss asked casually.

'No. As a matter of fact he didn't. Why do you ask, and would you mind telling me who I'm speaking to.'

'Not at all. My name is Edgar Hodgkiss.'

'You don't work at the IT Unit, do you? I've never heard Adrian mention any Hodgkiss.'

'No, Ms Rainer I don't work here. Actually Jan Campbell-Jones, the general manager of the council, and I are here this morning to try to work out what might have become of your brother.'

'Really?' Sarah inquired with no trace of alarm in her voice. 'And have you worked it out yet what … might have become of him?'

'At present we've no idea. It being Saturday we haven't yet had the opportunity to speak to any of his colleagues so we don't have much to work with. Would it be inconvenient if Ms Campbell-Jones and I were to call on you to discuss the matter of your brother's whereabouts in, say, half an hour; that is assuming you live locally.'

'I *do* live locally and you both should feel free to call on me as soon as you like.'

She gave Hodgkiss her address and hung up.

'And who was that?' Jan asked, re-entering the room holding a largish metal tray.

'That was Sarah Rainer, Whitten's sister. She has invited us to call on her as soon as we like.'

'Oh, and why should we do that?'

'Because I think it highly likely that she may be in a position to allow us access to the discs from the CCTV from this office. I think we would do well to familiarize ourselves with their contents. Wouldn't you agree?'

Jan nodded. 'An excellent idea, Hodgkiss. I'll just lay this tray over those suspicious looking marks in the drive way and let's not keep the lady waiting

*   *   *

The flat which Sarah Rainer shared with her brother was on the ground floor of an old-fashioned two-storey building near the railway station at Kylerbrin.

Hodgkiss plied the brass knocker on the door with vigour and the door was pulled open almost at once.

They were greeted by a good-looking woman of middle age. 'Mr Hodgkiss and Ms Campbell-Jones? Come in.'

They followed Sarah the length of the flat to a kitchen where there was a strong smell of coffee brewing.

She said over her shoulder, as she lifted a plate of sliced

cream cake from a shelf in a corner cupboard, 'if I seem less than distraught about my brother's unaccountable absence you must excuse me, but the truth is he was not a very likeable fellow.'

Hodgkiss asked curiously. 'Why did you speak of your brother in the past tense?'

'Did I do that? Really? I didn't notice. If I did I suppose it's because I've assumed he's dead.'

'That's a rather odd assumption, isn't it?' said Jan. 'He's only been missing a very little while. In fact you could hardly call it missing. Do you think he's dead just because he didn't come home last night?'

Sarah shook her head. 'Not, it's not that exactly. It's just a feeling I have. I can't explain it.'

'Well you may well be right,' said Hodgkiss. 'Ms Campbell-Jones and I have just finished examining his office and there is what I believe to be blood stains on the carpet in his office and on the concrete driveway near his external door.'

Sarah began pouring coffee from the percolator into three mugs. 'Everyone who knew him loathed him, you know.'

Hodgkiss nodded. 'Yes, so I've gathered. He certainly wasn't very popular at work.'

'And for good reason,' said Sarah, handing Jan a mug of coffee. 'He used to spy on them. I caught him once recently looking at vision from one of the CCTV cameras in their office.'

'Yes, we heard about that,' said Jan. 'Two of the staff having sex.'

'That's right. And of course he was holding it over their heads. He was just a nasty little tyrant. He used me like slave labour after my divorce and I was forced to come here to live.'

'Ms Campbell-Jones and I would be grateful if you could

find that vision from the CCTV. There may be a clue in that to what became of him.'

'You're using the past tense about him too, Mr Hodgkiss,' said Sarah. 'You think he's gone too, then, do you?'

Hodgkiss nodded. Yes, I believe so. Particularly since we found the blood. Of course the police will have to conduct tests and I may be wrong. But I think it's blood.'

Sarah pulled open a drawer under the kitchen bench and took out a plastic bag. She held it out to Hodgkiss. 'These are discs from the CCTV cameras. He only got them working again very recently and of course he never told the staff. The cameras hadn't been working for years before then.'

Hodgkiss took the bag. 'Do you know if he ever had any of the people in the Unit to do private work for him?'

'Yes. He had Eric Furlough re-wire this flat one weekend and he never paid the poor fellow a cent.'

Hodgkiss said: 'I noticed a new power point in Adrian's office. The one the big television set is plugged into. Do you know if Mr Furlough installed that?'

'Yes, he did. I happen to know because Adrian told me that he'd told Furlough off for using a white power point because it didn't blend with the dark woodwork. That's the sort of nitpicking sod he was … is. He told him he had no artistic taste. Called him a bogan. Not that the poor fellow would have cared what Adrian said about him. Those poor sods at that Unit … they all hated him.'

'You know that the staff had a winning ticket in the lottery … not a major prize but something substantial?'

'No. I'd no idea.'

'Adrian was holding out on them. He had refused to pass on their winnings.'

'Now there's a surprise. Perfectly in character with the

man. And another reason for someone to murder him.'

'I don't suppose you'd have any idea where he may have kept the ticket? I suppose he's not likely to leave it in his room or around the flat somewhere.'

Sarah shook her head. 'No. But I'll look around for it anyway, if you like. I'll look in his other suits and through his chest of drawers. If I find it I'll give you a ring. OK?'

*   *   *

'D'you mean to tell me that you've actually been out there ... to the council's IT unit?'

Seated at the round redwood table on the back deck of the family home Donald Burke looked angrily across at his father-in-law.

Hodgkiss was flabbergasted. 'Donald, I was not aware that you had the least interest in what had taken place at the Unit. In fact, as I recall, your last words to me on the subject were "can we just drop the whole thing." Or have you forgotten?'

'I haven't forgotten anything. *You* seem to have forgotten that I received a phone call from that place and that I responded in my capacity as a police investigator.'

'Yes, and your attitude after you'd been there, was that there was nothing to investigate; that nothing had happened that required any further police attention. And your crime scene officers did virtually nothing. Isn't that so?'

'No, it isn't so.'

'Very well, Donald. Then kindly tell me what you've done about the matter since then ... if anything?'

Donald shook his head angrily. 'It's not up to me to tell you anything. What I want to know ...'

It was at this point that Esme, who had heard the raised

voices from the kitchen, stepped out onto the deck.

'And what on earth are you two squabbling about now. The neighbours must be able to hear every word from three streets away. What's going on?'

'It's just your father up to his usual interfering tricks again,' said Donald, folding his arms across his chest.

'I see,' said Esme, turning to her father. 'I saw you go off with that woman from the council this morning. I might have known that no good would come of it.'

Esme had long objected to any contact between her father and Jan Campbell-Jones. So far as Esme was concerned Jan was altogether too fond of men. Stories of Jan's sexual exploits had come to Esme's ears and in spite of Hodgkiss' protests that they referred to Jan's distant past, Esme was unforgiving.

'A leopard doesn't change its spots, and that goes for female leopards too,' she had warned on more than one occasion.

'Now, Donald, what's this shouting about?' she demanded.

'It's just Dad up to his usual tricks, interfering again.'

'Interfering!" Hodgkiss exploded.

Esme snapped. 'That's enough, Dad. Can't I leave the two of you alone together for more than five minutes without you starting to squabble like two overgrown school boys? If you must argue can you please do it so half the neighbourhood can't hear you.'

She turned, stepped back inside and pulled the heavy sliding door closed behind her.

Hodgkiss resumed with an attempt at quiet reasonableness. 'Donald, I apologise if I have somehow trespassed on an active police investigation. If that is the case I am perfectly prepared to share with you the information Jan and I gathered during our visit to the Unit this morning.'

'Well, it shouldn't take long, should it? I mean there can't be a great deal of information to share, can there?'

Hodgkiss nodded agreeably. 'No, Not a great deal. Probably only the blood and the fact that …'

'Blood!' Donald barked, then clapped a hand over his mouth. He continued in more restrained tones. 'What blood? What on earth are you talking about? I didn't see any blood.'

'Ah, that's because you didn't expect to find any.'

'And you did?'

'I think I can honestly say that I expected to find some evidence of foul play in Whitten's office. It was, as you told me after your visit there, a mysterious locked room. And what's the most likely reason why someone takes the trouble to create a locked room situation? Our previous experience with these scenarios has been that they were designed to make a murder look like a suicide. Isn't that true?'

Donald nodded. 'Yes. I grant you that much. But you know as well as I that what at first looks like a blood stain often turns out to be something else altogether, often something quite innocuous. Right?'

'Perfectly true, Donald. I acknowledge that it may well turn out to be the case with the apparent blood stains on the carpet in Whitten's room and on the driveway outside the door. By the way, Jan took the sensible precaution of covering the stain on the driveway in case it rains.'

'So you're expecting me to turn up out there straightaway with a scientific team to test this alleged blood of yours. Is that what you're saying?'

Hodgkiss shrugged. 'Well, Donald, you'll have to make up your own mind about that, but I can tell you this; that the ill-will that exists between Whitten and the three members of his staff is likely to have generated some very strong emotions. And where you have an emotional tinder-box like that you have an impetus to violence. And then then is the gun shot to take into consideration.'

Donald shook his head. 'I'm not with you. What's this about tinder-boxes and ill-will? I don't know anything about any of that?'

'When you were there didn't you get a sense that all was not sweetness and light between the absent Whitten and the other three members of the staff?'

'No. There was nothing like that. They just seemed concerned that they'd heard a gun shot in their boss's room and couldn't understand why he wasn't in there when we broke down the door.

'In fact, come to think of it, I reckon they looked pretty puzzled when we realised the room was empty, but I suppose that was only to be expected since they thought they'd just heard a gunshot in there.'

'Did you ask if Mr Whitten could somehow have left the room after the shot?'

'Yes, and they were quite positive that there was no way he could have come out through their office without them noticing.'

'No doubt. But surely he could have left the room via that external door, rusty bolt or no rusty bolt.'

'But that's just not possible, Dad. I'm one hundred percent certain that the bolt on that external door was closed over in place when I broke into the room.

'He just couldn't have gone out that way after the shot. I mean, tell me, how would he go out the door then close the bolt on the inside?'

Hodgkiss stroked his well-trimmed grey beard thoughtfully. 'I think we must make a more thorough examination of that room, Donald. There must be more to learn about what happened there.

'Tell me, did you form an impression about the relationship between the staff at the Unit … how they got on?'

Donald shook his head. 'Not especially.'

'Then you're unaware that Whitten had surreptitiously obtained CCTV vision of Janice Evers and Eric Furlough having sex in their office after hours? Janice is married and Furlough is not. I have the discs from the Unit's CCTV cameras which I intend to watch, not out of prurience, mind you, but in case there is something else on those discs that might give a hint that will help us solve our little locked room mystery.

Hodgkiss continued. 'However, Whitten's sneaky little exercise in spying is not the only reason for discontent at the Unit. For some time the four of them had contributed regularly towards the cost of a lottery ticket and according to David Caton their latest ticket won a substantial prize and Whitten has refused to distribute their winnings.'

Donald grunted. 'I see. Then the three of them had a motive to do him harm. But I can't imagine them murdering him for a minor prize. Anyway, doing away with him wouldn't do them much good unless they could somehow get their hands on the winning lottery ticket.'

Hodgkiss nodded. 'Yes, that's true, Donald. But even so don't you think it might be worthwhile checking with the lottery people to see if that prize has been claimed and if it has, and the person who claimed it wasn't Whitten, then that will give us somewhere to take our investigation.'

'Yeah, I could do that, but I'd need the number of their ticket.'

Hodgkiss took out his tiny notebook. 'I believe I can help

you there.' He handed the notebook to Donald, pointing to an open page. 'I'm fairly sure the number of the winning ticket is the last number in that column.'

'And where did you get that?' Donald demanded. 'Making illegal searches of private property most likely,' he said in mock rebuke.

'Something like that,' Hodgkiss conceded. 'When Jan and I went to see Whitten's sister about getting the CCTV discs I also asked her if she'd seen the ticket. She has the misfortune to share a flat with her brother and she has promised to contact me if she finds the ticket, but somehow I doubt if she will discover it in the flat.'

'OK then. I'll check to see if this ticket's been presented and I'll get the scene of crime boys to go back and have a look at this alleged blood you reckon's on the carpet and in the driveway. Satisfied?'

'I am confident that it will not prove to be a waste of police resources,' said Hodgkiss.

*   *   *

As Rolf approached, Whitten was standing unsteadily in the driveway, swaying slightly from side to side.

Then he turned and looked directly at Rolf. 'It's Friday afternoon?' he said in a loud clear voice, ending the sentence with an upward inflection.

Rolf answered almost without thinking. 'Yes sir. That's right, it's Friday afternoon. Your car's waiting over there.'

'My car?' Whitten muttered. 'My car's waiting? Yes. Where am I going?'

'You have an important meeting, sir?'

'Yes of course. My meeting. Where? Where's the meeting?'

"You'll remember all about it when we get there,' said Rolf, laying a firm hand on Whitten's shoulder and turning him towards the road.

It was then that he noticed the small section of damp, matted hair on the side of Whitten's head.

That looks like blood, he thought with alarm as he steered Whitten towards the car.

In his haste to reach the car Rolf failed to notice a small black remote control slip from Whitten's belt onto the driveway.

When they reached the car Rolf opened the back door and lowered Whitten into a sitting position. He picked up some pages from an old newspaper on the floor of the compartment, spread them on the seat then he lowered Whitten down with his bloodied head resting on the paper. Then he bundled his legs and feet into the car and closed the door.

He walked unhurriedly around the car, opened the driver's door and slid behind the wheel. He started the motor, checked the wing mirror for traffic, then pulled out from the curb and drove slowly away.

He drove with more than usual caution through the northern suburbs of Kanundda, being careful to stay within the speed limit. When in the city Rolf usually drove with one eye, his left eye, tightly closed. This was because his squint, which had worsened in recent years, now caused double vision. At first he had been able to control his focus by sheer concentration. But lately it had become unmanageable and whenever he drove with both eyes open the road ahead appeared to be intersected at an angle of about thirty degrees by a second phantom roadway which could be eliminated only by closing one eye.

Twenty minutes later he turned onto the Kanundda Head

Road and slowed the car, searching the surrounding bush for a spot that would offer concealment. He soon found a deserted spot shielded from the road by a group of dense shrubs. He pulled over onto a rutted dirt track and stopped the car, satisfied that he was not visible to passing motorists.

He climbed out and opened the rear door. Leaning in he began an examination of his passenger.

Whitten's breathing was regular but shallow. He appeared to be asleep and since the newspaper showed no trace of staining he assumed that any bleeding had stopped.

'Mr Whitten,' Rolf said softly.

There was no response.

'Adrian,' he said in a louder voice.

Whitten's eyes flew wide open.

'Yes, I'm Adrian,' he said clearly, then asked: 'Am I going to a meeting?'

'Yes, but we've had to stop on the way.'

Whitten's eyes closed again.

Cautiously Rolf slipped a hand into Whitten's inside jacket pocket and drew out a thick black leather wallet. He rifled quickly through the compartments until he found the lottery ticket. He extracted it and four fifty dollar notes which he placed in his slack's pocket. then he returned the wallet to Whitten's jacket.

He closed the rear door and climbed back into the driver's seat.

Now, what the hell am I going to do with this bastard, he thought. I'll have to cash the lottery ticket before he gets his act together, so where can I park him safely until then?

Then he remembered that his sister had exchanged house keys with a neighbour to be used in some emergency if the other was absent from home.

He started the motor and backed cautiously out of the bush and onto the road. Twenty minutes later he backed the car into his own garage and lowered the door.

Luckily he remembered where Janice had told him the neighbour's key could be found and after a short search he hurried next door to look for a suitable private and secure place to deposit Whitten while he attended to the business of claiming on the lottery ticket.

Firstly, he inspected the neighbour's carport which offered concealment on three sides. From the carport there was a door which opened into a double garage.

Then he remembered that Janice had mentioned that the neighbours, a couple by the name of Moss, would be away for some time on a European holiday.

One of the keys on the ring opened the garage door. Two cars were parked in the garage. Rolf concluded that the Mosses must have taken a taxi to the airport when they left for their holiday.

Rolf left the garage side door ajar then returned to his own garage. He raised the door, drove out into the street then backed up the neighbour's driveway into the carport. Once there he opened the rear door nearest the open garage door and man-handled Whitten, now apparently comatose, into the Moss's garage where he laid him on his side on the cement floor.

Rolf was uncertain how long it would take him to claim on the ticket so he decided it would be necessary to immo-bilize Whitten lest he should wake.

He looked about. An old pair of jeans was hanging on a nail nearby. A wide leather belt was threaded through the loops in the jean's waist. Rolf pulled the belt free and with it he bound Whitten's hands securely together behind his back.

That'll hold you for a while, you bastard, he thought. He

stepped back into the carport and pulled the garage door closed behind him.

Rolf had already researched the location of the lottery office nearest to the Unit and it was there that he drove. The young woman to whom he presented the ticket accepted it without comment and disappeared through a door in the rear wall.

Within minutes she returned. 'Do you have your registration,' she asked with a bored expression.

Rolf cursed silently. He said; 'I thought I might be able to just pick up our prize. That's what we all want.'

The young woman simply shook her head. 'You'll need your registration before I can pay out. If you're not registered you'll have to fill in a claim form and post it in. You can download the form off our web site,' she said and turned away.

Now matters had become seriously complicated. It appeared that somehow he would have to secure Whitten's cooperation in finding this registration document, whatever it was.

He returned to the car and drove slowly home once more. But instead of turning into his own drive he once more reversed up the Moss's drive and stopped in the carport.

He opened the door into the garage cautiously, fearing that Whitten may have recovered and finding himself trussed perhaps had broken free and was prepared to make a stand against his captor.

But he need not have worried. Whitten lay as he had left him; on his side, hands bound behind his back.

Now, what am I going to do with him, Rolf thought. First of all I'm going to have to find out from him where this registration paperwork is. When I've got that it should be smooth sailing.

Then it occurred to him that Whitten's sister may have the document he needed.

Then he thought, perhaps the registration papers are in his wallet and I just didn't recognise them. He knelt down and reached again into the inside pocket of the jacket.

But there was nothing in Whitten's wallet that resembled a lottery registration paper.

He thought, I'll ask him about it when he comes around and gets his wits together. Meanwhile, he decided, it would be safe to leave Whitten there for the night and he could return first thing in the morning to see if he had regained his senses.

When he left to return next door Rolf decided to leave his car in the Moss's car port. If anyone asked him about it he could say that he'd left it there to give the impression that the house was still occupied as a deterrent to burglary.

But when he returned the next morning Whitten was still unconscious and his breathing, while still shallow, was quite regular.

The following day, after he returned from work, he went next door again to check on Whitten. When he opened the garage door and went inside he saw at once that Whitten had been stirring. He had rolled over onto the other side and his wrists appeared to have chaffed, probably where he had tried to escape from the belt.

Also he had knocked over two cans of paint, white and grey. These had spilled across the garage floor, around the tyres of one of the cars and had stained the cuffs of Whitten's pants.

Rolf cursed but decided it was not necessary for him to do anything about the mess. He simply righted the overturned cans, which had spilled most of their contents, and wiped his hands on a cloth hanging from a nail nearby.

When he had done this he once more turned his attention to Whitten who was lying quietly.

Too quietly, Rolf decided.

Then with a shock he realised that Whitten did not appear to be breathing.

He froze beside the still, silent form and listened.

Nothing.

He leaned down and placed a finger on the wrist below where the belt bound it.

Again nothing. And the skin was quite cool. Cooler than it should have been because the inside of the garage was uncomfortably warm.

The bastard's gone and died on me.

Now, what the hell am I going to do with him?

*   *   *

On Monday evening Hodgkiss was waiting impatiently in the kitchen for Donald to arrive home.

'For heavens' sake, Dad,' said Esme, 'don't hang around here waiting to pounce on the poor man as soon as he sets foot inside the house. Go out on the back deck and read your book. I'll let him know you want to talk to him … as if he wouldn't already know.'

It was nearly half an hour before Donald, can of beer in hand, pulled back the heavy sliding door from the family room and stepped out onto the deck.

Hodgkiss looked up from where he was reading at the redwood table. 'Any progress yet on our little investigation?'

'I don't know if you'd call it progress,' said Donald, sitting down heavily on the curved bench seat opposite Hodgkiss. 'I'd be more inclined to call it movement, if anything.'

'Very well. And in which direction has this movement taken us?'

'Well this morning early … and I mean really early … about five a.m., a woman by the name of Sarah Rainer, who claimed to be Adrian Whitten's sister, rang to say her brother had disappeared. She said he didn't come home on Friday night and she hasn't seen or heard from him since. She said it's most unusual for him to go missing like that. I've sent a constable out to take a statement from her. The constable who took the call said she sounded pretty casual about it all. Also she asked how long a person had to be missing before they could be declared legally dead. Not exactly the attitude you'd expect from a caring blood relation.'

Hodgkiss nodded. 'Which brings us neatly to the question of the other blood, the blood I … we found in Whitten's office and on the driveway near his side door. Any word on that?'

'Give us a break, Dad. You know very well the sorts of tests the lab boys have to make before they can say for sure that something is definitely human blood.'

'Yes, Donald, I know all about that. But did they express a preliminary opinion?'

'Well I can tell you that the scene-of-crime boys who took the samples reckoned the patches on the floor and in the drive-way *looked* like blood but they weren't going to be held to it.

'When I told them about how I discovered the room was locked up tight they made a bit of a joke about it. They reckoned that if it *was* blood then it'd have to be the blood of a ghost seeing that there was no way in or out of the room.'

Hodgkiss nodded. 'That is indeed our problem, Donald. And not one that will be easily solved until we can identify whose blood it is and the relationship between that person and the members of the Unit staff.'

'Then you reckon that if Whitten's come to some harm then it's his pals in the Unit who are most likely responsible?'

'I doubt if there is any basis for referring to the others who work there as Whitten's "pals". Anyway, that aside, would you like to know what I found on the CCTV tapes.'

'I expect there wasn't much you could talk about in polite company. Not in any detail anyway. After all, that was how Whitten got onto his two staff members having it off … caught them on the CCTV, wasn't it?'

Hodgkiss shook his head indignantly. 'Donald, if you are implying that I have spent my time taking a voyeuristic interest in the activities of that unfortunate couple, then I bitterly resent it. As it happens there were more interesting things to see than that.'

'Really? Like what?'

'Why don't you come and see for yourself. I would be interested to hear what you make of it.'

Hodgkiss rose from his bench and lead the way back inside. In his bedroom Hodgkiss sat at his computer and with a touch of the mouse brought the screen to life.

He said: 'This is vision from the CCTV on the Saturday before the Friday when the gunshot was heard in Whitten's office.'

On the screen was a still image of Eric Furlough standing in what Donald recognised as the main office at the Unit. He was carrying what appeared to be a length of white-coated electrical wire coiled around his shoulder. In one hand he held a hammer and in the other hand two tools which could not be identified due to the grainy vision.

Hodgkiss touched a button on his computer and on the screen Furlough lips moved as if he was speaking to someone who was not in the picture. Then he walked to the right of the screen and disappeared from sight.

Hodgkiss touched a button and the screen froze.

He turned to Donald. 'Well, what do you make of that?'

Donald shrugged. 'Not a lot. What do *you* make of it?'

'Well, now we know that about a week before the gunshot in Whitten's office, Furlough, one of the two people who had been under some pressure from Whitten, went into Whitten's office at the weekend. He carried with him some electricians lead and some tools.'

'Yeah. Well that was obvious. But what did he do with them?'

Hodgkiss held up a hand. 'As they say in the advertising world: "But wait … there's more."'

Again he touched a key on his computer's keyboard and the tape went into fast forward mode. Hodgkiss, who had been following a counter on the screen, suddenly touched another key and the screen came to life. The counter showed that about half an hour had passed. Furlough re-entered the office from the right of the screen. But this time he was carrying an apparently diminished loop of electrician's wire and the tools apparently had been discarded.

Janice Evers came into the picture from the left of the screen and there was a short conversation before Furlough disappeared again off the right of the screen and Janice went to a desk, pulled open the top drawer and drew out some object too small to identify.

Hodgkiss explained. 'I believe the item Ms Evers is holding is similar to one of those remote control devices used for raising and lowering garage doors. I saw it in her desk when Jan and I visited the Unit on Saturday.'

'So what do you reckon she uses it for?' Donald asked.

Hodgkiss shrugged. 'I've no idea. But watch what happens now.'

On the screen Janice raised her arm to the right of the screen.

Hodgkiss said. 'She is now pointing the remote in the direction of Whitten's office.'

After about ten seconds Janice lowered her arm and held the remote by her side, apparently waiting.

Almost at once Furlough re-entered from the right of the picture, smiling broadly. He gave a thumbs up sign.

Janice placed the remote in the top drawer of her desk and the two disappeared off the screen to the left.

'And what do you think that was all about?' Donald asked.

Hodgkiss hesitated before replying. 'I'm not sure, but it could have had something to do with the new wiring Furlough installed for Whitten to plug in his massive new TV set, but I doubt it. I'd say he did that earlier.'

'Any ideas, then?'

'Yes, I have an idea, but as yet it is extremely nebulous.'

'Too nebulous to even talk about, I suppose.'

Hodgkiss nodded. 'Donald, you should know my methods by now. I am loath to lay my cards on the table before I have filled my hand.'

'And how long will it be before you've filled your hand, d'you think?'

'There are a number of pieces of critical information missing before the jigsaw can be completed and the full picture becomes clear.'

Donald signed. As usual the old bugger was going to be difficult. 'OK. So where do we go from here?'

'I think one issue that must be clarified is whether or not

there has been an attempt made to collect on the winning lottery ticket.'

'And how do you plan to do that? There must be thousands of places in this city where you can collect on a ticket … just about every newsagent sells the things.'

'Granted. But this would not be an ordinary transaction. It was not a prize that could be collected in cash over the counter at any newsagent.'

'I don't see that that makes any difference,' said Donald. 'You'd still have to check out every newsagent in town.'

'Very well, Donald. I see that as usual it is going to be left to me to progress the matter. So be it.'

Hodgkiss turned off his computer and left the room abruptly. Five minutes later Donald found Hodgkiss slouched in the uncomfortable director's chair on the back deck.

'OK, Dad,' he said. 'I'll see what I can do about the ticket. But it won't happen in a hurry. Satisfied?'

'I suppose I'll have to be,' said Hodgkiss with poor grace. But he had decided already to pursue the matter himself.

*　　　*　　　*

Early the next morning Hodgkiss booted up his computer and opened the email. He wrote —

to jcampbell-jones@kanunddacouncil.com.au

I am anxious to know whether or not there has been any attempt to claim on the ticket shared by the staff at your IT Unit. Is there any way of finding out from any of the surviving members of that place? I would anticipate that putting that question to either Janice Evers or Furlough would not likely be productive, however David Caton may have information on the matter which he may be prepared to pass on. I say this because I am confident that he was not involved in whatever it was that befell the late unlamented Adrian Whitten.

EH

Email to <u>ehodgkiss@ozemail.com.au</u>

"Late unlamented". Then obviously you are of the view that Whitten is no longer in the land of the living. Upon reflection I must say I agree with you.

I will, as you ask, put your question to young David Caton with your request. It would be best to ask him to come to my office on some pretext where I can go into the matter with him one-on-one, because if your suspicions about his two remaining workmates are justified, then the less they know about my interest in their ticket the better. I will be in touch when there is something to report.

JC-J

But Hodgkiss decided not to wait for a result from that quarter. He pushed back from his computer and hurried down the hall to the kitchen where Esme was packing the dishwasher with the utensils from their breakfast.

'Would you have time to drive me to a certain destination in West Lillimoor this morning?' he asked.

'West Lillimoor?' said Esme 'Why on earth do you want to go there?'

Hodgkiss sighed dramatically. 'If it is too much trouble for you, Esme, just say so. There are other modes of transport available.

Esme shook her head in frustration. Her father's reference to 'other modes of transport' was his usual means of cajoling her into giving him a lift by threatening to ring for a cab, a manoeuvre which he knew always resulted in her agreeing to drive him where he wished to go.

'I suppose I could do my shopping at West Lillimoor, although the prices at shops down there are twice as expensive as the supermarket.'

Hodgkiss observed. 'I think the supermarket will survive for just one day without your custom.'

Ten minutes later Esme was backing the small family sedan into a parking spot outside a newsagent in the small cluster of shops at West Lillimoor. 'Will this be convenient for sir?' she asked caustically.

'Perfect,' said Hodgkiss climbing out of the car. 'I should be only a few minutes.'

'Well, I might be a good deal longer than that, so you can just wait in the car,' said Esme, heading for a convenience store nearby.

Hodgkiss entered the newsagent and made for that section of the counter which housed the equipment where lottery tickets were checked.

As a young woman approached Hodgkiss took from his pocket a scrap of paper on which he had written the number of the Unit's winning ticket.

He turned on his most winning smile. 'I'm frightfully sorry to bother you, but I was wondering if you could help me. It's about a ticket that won a prize lately, a biggish prize. Too big to be paid out across the counter.' He held out the scrap of paper. 'That's the number of the ticket,' he said hopefully.

The young woman gave the paper a cursory glance. 'Do you really think that I remember the numbers of all the tickets that pass through here?'

'No of course not' said Hodgkiss quickly. 'I just thought that it might be a bit unusual for someone to present a ticket here for one of the bigger prizes.'

She shrugged. 'When that happens they usually just send it straight to the head office and they post out the cheque.'

'Then you haven't had anyone come in recently trying to claim one of the bigger prizes over the counter?'

'I didn't say that,' said the girl querulously.

'Then may I take it that you have?'

'Yes. The other day in fact.'

'I don't suppose you know who it was, do you. Were they regulars who buy their tickets here.'

'No. and it was just one person … a man.'

'And could you describe this man?'

The young woman gave that some thought. 'He was small. He was pretty overweight and he had these really creepy eyes.'

'Creepy eyes. Creepy in what way?' Hodgkiss asked.

'Well, one eye would be looking straight at you and the other one would be looking over there,' said the young woman, pointing towards the street.

Hodgkiss nodded. 'And do you remember anything else about him. Did he speak with an accent? What colour was his hair?'

The girl frowned. 'Why are you asking all these questions? I'm not allowed to give out personal information about our customers, you know.'

Hodgkiss nodded. 'Oh I realise that, but thank you anyway.'

He turned and left the shop. Outside he sat on a wooden bus stop seat and took out his mobile phone.

In her office at the front of the Kanundda Council Chambers building Jan Campbell-Jones cursed as her tiny blue mobile phone broke into its ringtone, a tinny rendition of The Ride of the Valkyries.

She picked up the phone and glanced and the caller ID.

'Yes, Hodgkiss. What is it? I'm actually busy with council business, believe it or not.'

'One very simple question,' said Hodgkiss.

'That'll be a first,' Jan muttered. 'All right. What is it … this simple question?'

'Do you know anyone who fits the following description: small, pretty overweight and with creepy eyes?'

'Creepy eyes. Can you elaborate?'

'Yes. He had a distinct cast in his eyes. One eye looks straight ahead and the other looks off at a tangent.'

'No one springs to mind. But why are you ringing me? Unless of course it's in connection with events at the Unit and Whitten's disappearance.'

'Of course it is, and the description I have just given you was provided less than five minutes ago by a young lady at the news agency not three minutes walk from the Unit. That was her recollection of a man who attempted to collect their lottery prize.'

At her desk Jan nodded. 'Now I see. OK. Well, I can tell you that the description you have given rings no bells with me, but I will contact the fellow who runs our HR services. He's been with us for many years and I'd say he has a fairly extensive knowledge of all of our personnel. I'll call back.'

Hodgkiss had been waiting on the seat for less than five minutes when his phone rang.

It was Jan. 'Your man's name is Rolf Evers.'

'A close relation of Janice Evers, no doubt.'

'Her brother I'm given to understand. But that would have to be checked.'

'I doubt if checking will be necessary. All that needs to be checked is the part which the Evers family played in the death and disappearance of Adrian Whitten.'

'Yes. It would be hard to argue with that. What do you think happened?'

'As I have just explained to Donald, I am not yet in possession of all the essential facts and in order to obtain them I think a further inspection of the Unit's premises will be necessary. I have not yet been able to make sense of the happenings which we saw on the CCTV, therefore may we meet once more at the IT Unit tomorrow … and unfortunately I think on this occasion it will be necessary for Donald also to be in attendance.'

Jan glanced at her diary which stood in leather frame on her desk. 'I've got an hour or two free first thing tomorrow. I'll call for you at 8.30. Is that too early?'

'By no means,' Hodgkiss replied. 'I will be waiting on the nature strip.'

That evening, after dinner, Hodgkiss joined Donald on the back deck. 'Donald, would it be too much trouble for you to visit the IT Unit tomorrow morning at, say, 9 o'clock.'

Donald looked up from the local newspaper. 'And why on earth should I visit the IT Unit at 9 o'clock tomorrow?'

'Because I believe that Jan and I are making progress in our investigation into what took place there and I thought you might like to share in any new discoveries.'

'Really?' said Donald sceptically. 'Then may I take it that you have filled your hand and are about to lay your cards on the table?'

'That is the purpose of my visit, Donald. I hope to fill my hand. I intend to test a particular theory which I have developed since you and I last discussed this matter. If things turn out as I anticipate I will be in a position to demonstrate how the extraordinary situation of an empty locked room was arranged.'

'Will you really,' said Donald. 'Well, I must say that sounds like something I wouldn't miss for quids ... that is if it actually happens. OK. Nine o'clock you say ... at the Unit. I'll be there.'

*   *   *

Jan was waiting at the kerb in her council car when Hodgkiss hurried down the front path.

'Donald will be joining us about nine,' he announced, climbing into the car and fastening his seat belt. 'I promised that I'd demonstrate for him how they did the trick with the locked room.'

Jan turned to look at Hodgkiss with amazement. 'That was rather rash, wasn't it? Anyway, who is "they"? Are you telling me you know who's responsible for ... whatever it is that's happened to Adrian Whitten?'

'Really, Jan,' said Hodgkiss tartly. 'Do you really need to ask that? Janice Evers and Eric Furlough are responsible. Who else could it be?'

'All right, but exactly what are they responsible for?'

Hodgkiss held up a cautionary finger. 'Ahha. Now that is indeed the pertinent question.' He slipped into didactic mode. 'Actually there are two questions to be considered; the first one being who conceived, planned and created the locked room scenario and for what purpose; and the second is, what became of Whitten after the gunshot that was heard, apparently, in his room?'

'That sounds like three questions to me,' said Jan, smiling.

'Don't split hairs. Now, my answer to the first question, which I hope to prove shortly, is that the naughty Janice and her lover between them devised the method to create the locked room situation which Donald discovered when he came here in response to Janice's call about the gunshot in Whitten's office.

'And as for the section question, what happened to Whitten after the shot was heard, I cannot say, although there are several strong indications.'

Five minutes later Jan turned into the driveway beside the IT Unit and drove to the rear of the building where she parked in a space marked "Manager". The three other marked parking spaces were vacant.

Jan said. 'I've told the three of them to work out of head office today on the assumption that you wouldn't want them around while you … do whatever you're going to do.'

'That was very thoughtful of you, Jan, as always. Now, I take it you have brought the keys.'

Jan dangled a bunch of keys from her index finger.

'Excellent.' Hodgkiss followed as Jan led the way up the back steps and into the building.

In the middle of the main office she stood, hands on hips 'OK, Hodgkiss. Where do we start?'

'The object of our exercise here today is, as I have said, to establish how Whitten exited from his office at the same time managing to leave the door from his room to this office both locked and bolted on the inside and with the bolt on the door leading out to the driveway also firmly in place after he departed.'

Jan nodded. 'That sounds like a pretty tall order. So what do we do?'

Hodgkiss crossed to one of the desks standing against the side wall nearest the driveway. He pulled open the top drawer and drew out a black plastic remote.

Jan asked: 'It that the thing we saw Janice holding on the CCTV?'

Hodgkiss nodded. 'I believe so.'

'And what does it do? Turn on the television in Whitten's office?'

'I doubt that very much. But I've no doubt that it does operate *something* in Whitten's office. Did you notice on the CCTV that when Furlough entered Whitten's office he was carrying a length of what appeared to be white-coated electricians' flex coiled over his shoulder?'

'Yes. And he was carrying it when he came out again.'

Hodgkiss nodded. 'Correct. And when he went in he was also carrying what looked like tools, including a hammer. Right?'

'Yes, and he didn't bring them out again.'

'The CCTV didn't show him bringing them out but I've no doubt that he would have recovered them before Whitten came to work the next day.'

OK. But what about them?'

'Obviously he needed them for some purpose, and I've got a pretty good idea what it was. I'll need that remote to show you what I mean.'

Jan handed the remote to Hodgkiss just as they heard a car drive into the parking area at the rear.

'That will be Donald,' said Hodgkiss crossing to the back door. He was in time to see Donald park the unmarked police car in the marked space beside Jan's car.

He turned to Jan who was standing beside him. 'I don't suppose he'll have anything worthwhile to report. Things don't work at meteoric speed in the police force, I'm afraid.'

However in this Hodgkiss was mistaken. When Donald joined them in the main office Hodgkiss was about to launch into a summary of the events disclosed on the CCTV camera when Donald held up a hand.

'Before you start on that, Dad, there's something you should know. We've found Whitten.'

'Dead or alive?' Hodgkiss asked quickly.

'Very dead. Shot in the head. A bushwalker found his body beside a fire trail in the Kanundda National Park about three hundreds yards off the Kanundda Head Road.'

'Do we know how long he'd been there?'

'Less than two days. The guy who found him said he walked over that part of the trail two days earlier and he wasn't there then.'

'And do we know when he died?'

'Only approximately. The doctor said he'd been dead no more than three days.

'So he could have been dead before he was dumped there? Doesn't help much does it?'

Jan said. 'It means he didn't die for up to three days after he was shot. Is that possible? Do we know if he was given any sort of medical attention after being shot?'

Donald shook his head. 'No. I checked on that and there's no record or sign of him receiving medical treatment for the wound or any report of him attending any hospital or doctor's surgery in the area, and if he had they would have been sure to report treating a bullet wound in the head. And another thing; he had the gun in his pocket.'

Hodgkiss asked: 'Was it the gun used to shoot him?'

'Very likely. Forensics reckon it looks like the right calibre although they haven't had time yet to finish all the tests. And his fingerprints are on it.'

'Are there any other prints?' Hodgkiss asked.

'No. Nothing.'

'Well, that doesn't come as a surprise, does it? This is indeed an extremely complex matter and in order to understand ...'

But Donald cut him off angrily. 'Look, Dad, if you reckon you know what happened here let's have it and none of your beating around the bush this time; none of this not saying anything 'til you've filled your ruddy hand or any nonsense like that. I've run out of patience with that kind of stuff. You either know or you don't.'

'Very well, Donald. Then let us cut to the chase. Let's tackle the first question; after he'd been shot in the head how did Adrian Whitten contrive to leave this room in such a way that it was locked up behind him when he had gone. Because that's what must have happened, do you agree?'

'I guess so,' Donald conceded unwillingly.

Hodgkiss nodded. 'Good. Now we know he was in his office when two members of the staff in this room heard a shot. Apparently concerned at what might have happened Janice Evers contacted police … yourself. She did this because they could not attract his attention by banging on the door and they could not gain access to his room via either door or the window. Nor could they see in.

'You arrived here *poste haste* and, in the belief that prompt action may save the man's life, you broke down that door.'

Hodgkiss paused, pointing to the door between the main room and Whitten's office. 'But when you forced entry to the office it was empty. Not only was it empty but it was at once evident that both doors to the room had been bolted shut and the window, too, was locked in place.'

'Yeah, yeah we know all of that,' Donald snapped testily. 'Now are you going to come to the point and tell us something we don't know, like how it was done, because if not I'm going back to the station because there's plenty of fair dinkum work to do there.'

Hodgkiss held up a hand. 'Patience, Donald. I am coming

to the point, which is this; how is it possible that there was no one in the room when you broke in? I think the answer to that is best given by a simple demonstration of what happened.

'I will go into Whitten's office now, close the door and then, give me thirty seconds then I want you to come in and find me. All right?'

'It sounds to me like another one of your silly games to me,' said Donald.

'OK, Hodgkiss,' said Jan. 'Stop talking and get on with it.'

Hodgkiss entered Whitten's office, turned and closed the door behind him. From the other side of the door he called: 'Now pretend that this door is locked and bolted. Thirty seconds, then come in.'

Donald pulled back his left cuff and followed the sweep second hand on his watch. Then he stepped forward, turned the handle and pushed open the door Hodgkiss had closed only seconds earlier.

He and Jan stepped into an empty office.

At once Donald hurried across to the door leading to the driveway.

But it too was locked and the large iron bolt was shot across in place.

He stood at the door, staring at the bolt, baffled. Then he turned to Jan. 'How the hell did he do that?'

'Easy,' said Hodgkiss, who was now standing behind them at the door to the outer office, leaning casually against the architrave.

'OK, Hodgkiss,' said Jan. 'Let's have it … how did you do it?'

'It wasn't rocket science. All the clues were there in the CCTV … the length of white-coated electrician's wire … the tools Furlough was carrying … the remote … the thumbs up sign signifying that the arrangement had worked.'

'And exactly what arrangement was that?' Jan snapped, now out of patience.

'Come with me and I'll show you.' Hodgkiss crossed Whitten's office to the side door leading to the driveway.

He reached up and pulled the bolt back. Then he put a hand in his slack's pocket and moments later the bolt flew across into its housing in the door jamb.

'C'mon, Dad. What have you got there?' said Donald indicating Hodgkiss' pocket.

Hodgkiss' hand came out of the pocket holding the small black remote. 'Watch', he said. He reached up and pulled back the bolt. When he released it it flew back once more into its socket.

'As I said, it wasn't rocket science, but there was *some* science involved. Going back to what we saw on the CCTV; during the time that Furlough spent in this room he inserted a small but powerful electromagnet in the architrave of this door, level with the bolt.

'It was the bolt that first caught my attention and set me wondering. You see, it was rusty, so it probably was made of iron, a magnetic metal, rather than stainless steel which is usually used for these items.

'First Furlough ran some electric cable under the roof and down the cavity wall to a point where he could connect the electromagnet.

'Remember that he was skilled in electronics so it was a simple matter for him to arrange a radio-controlled switch, similar to that used for a garage door, to turn the electro-magnet on and off.'

Donald nodded. 'OK. So that's how they made the whole thing look like a locked room. But what was the point of it?'

'The point of it, Donald, is that Mrs Evers and Furlough

planned to murder that ghastly man and create a scenario where the police would logically assume that Whitten had committed suicide.'

Jan asked: 'Then you say it was Janice Evers and Eric Furlough who were responsible … who shot him?'

'Of course. It had to be them. They were the only ones in a position to make the necessary arrangements. Besides, we have the evidence of the CCTV.'

Donald cut in. 'But that's nonsense, Dad. Why go to the trouble of setting up all these elaborate electrical gimmicks then cart him off and dump him in the Kanundda National Park.'

Hodgkiss shook his head in dismay. 'Really, Donald, sometimes I have no hope for you. What on earth led you to believe that it was Janice Evers and Furlough who dumped him in the national park.'

'Well, if it wasn't them who was it? Or haven't you filled your hand on that one yet?'

'Yes, Donald, my hand is full and I am now prepared to lay my cards on the table. But first, have you been able to ascertain as yet if there has been any attempt to present the group's winning ticket?'

Donald shook his head. 'No, Dad. And I wasn't prepared to send half the office off on a wild goose chase to try and do something that would have taken weeks and even then they probably would never have got a result.'

'Indeed!' said Hodgkiss. 'Then you'll be surprised to learn that I have already located the culprit.'

'The hell you have,' said Donald, unable to conceal his amazement. 'And how on earth did you do that?'

'It was not difficult at all. I simply went on the assumption that if the ticket was presented it would have been presented by one of the three remaining people in the group that contributed towards it. Next, I asked myself where was the most likely place they would go to present it. And of course the logical answer was, at the nearest agency, where the ticket was purchased. So I went there. It's just a few minutes down the road. When I made my inquiry the young lady who works there said that someone *had* presented the ticket and asked for the prize. When told about the procedure that had to be followed the person left hurriedly.'

'And which one of them was it?' Donald demanded.

'It was none of them,' Hodgkiss admitted simply.

'But you just said that ...' Donald began.

'Yes, and I was wrong.'

'Then who was it?'

'A man by the name of Rolf Evers. Janice Evers' brother.'

'And you reckon it was this Rolf Evers that murdered Whitten?'

'I do not believe anything of the kind,' said Hodgkiss indignantly.

'But wasn't the whole point of finding out who presented the ticket to establish who it was that took it from Whitten after he'd been shot. That was the idea, wasn't it?'

'Yes, Donald that's true. But it wasn't Rolf Evers who shot Whitten.'

Donald shook his head. 'Dad, you're beginning to lose me.'

'You lost me some time ago, Hodgkiss,' said Jan. 'So what happened here. Do you really know?'

Hodgkiss shook his head. 'I don't really *know* in the sense that I could prove it in a court of law. Nevertheless I believe I *do* know.'

'Well, let's have that at least,' said Donald.

'Very well. Now that we know the mechanics of what

happened here with the electronic bolt we can proceed from the point where Furlough has shot Whitten in the head. He then placed the gun in Whitten's hand to suggest suicide, locked and bolted the door to the outer office then he left via the side door, down the driveway and returned to the main office.

'He activated the electromagnet closing the bolt in the side door thus completely sealing the room.

'Then Janice Evers rang you, Donald, to say that they heard a shot and were concerned for Whitten' safety. They stressed how they could not enter the room or see through the window and in spite of all their efforts they could not attract his attention, or so they told you in tones of the greatest urgency no doubt.

'And that was the situation you found when you arrived.

'Now what must have happened was this; although mortally wounded Whitten was not dead.

'Almost immediately after being shot he got up from where he had fallen, leaving some blood stains on the carpet.

'Now this is important. When he got up he had the gun in his hand because, as I said earlier, Furlough had placed it there so that when the police broke into the room his death would appear to have been a suicide, which, after all, was the point of all the elaborate arrangements to create a locked room.

'But although he was mortally wounded, Whitten nevertheless continued to operate at some level of consciousness.

'While this condition is rare it is certainly not unknown. A quick search on the internet will bear this out. There are credible reports of people with mortal head wounds surviving actively for days after being shot.

'Once on his feet Whitten attempted at once to get clear of the place where he had been attacked.

'But he did not want to go out through the outer office where he knew his attacker would intercept him and finish the job. So he went to the side door.

'He pulled back the bolt, pushed the door open and stepped out into the driveway.

'When he closed the door the bolt immediately flew back into place because the power to the electromagnet had not been turned off.'

Donald protested. 'Dad, you can't possibly know all this.'

'Donald, I do not claim to *know* anything. I thought I had already made that point clear.

'OK. So what do you reckon happened next?'

'It is at this point that matters become rather more speculative. But since it was Janice Evers' brother Rolf who gained possession of the ticket I am assuming that it was he who somehow met and possibly intercepted and abducted Whitten. That is the best explanation I can advance for Whitten's disappearance and Evers being in possession of the ticket.

'I believe that Evers held Whitten prisoner somewhere for a number of days before he died and his body deposited in the national park.

'Whitten must have been in possession of the gun when Evers spotted him. It would have been necessary to disarm him although later, after Whitten died, Rolf could have simply returned the gun by placing it in his pocket, taking care not to leave his fingerprints on it.'

'Now, Donald, whatever you may think of my theory, I would strongly suggest that an interview with Rolf Evers and a search of his premises would be the very least you can do.'

Donald shrugged. 'Can't do any harm I guess.'

'And I wouldn't leave it too long. He may not be the

sharpest tool in the shed but I'd say that even he, given enough time, could cover his tracks sufficiently well to make a conviction difficult.'

'Then let's not stand around talking about it,' said Donald. 'I suppose you know where this Evers guy lives, do you?'

Hodgkiss nodded. 'Yes. I suggest you follow Jan and I,' he said.

Five minutes later Jan stopped her sedan across the road from the modest bungalow which Rolf Evers shared with his sister.

But their attention was caught at once by a police car, lights flashing, stopped outside the neighbouring house where a police constable stood in the car port talking on his mobile phone.

Donald hurried up the driveway, Hodgkiss and Jan close behind him.

On seeing Donald approaching the constable ended his conversation and came to attention.

'What's the problem here, Constable Brooks?' Donald asked.

'We had a call from the lady who owns this place,' the constable replied. 'The family, name of Moss, was away on holidays but one of the kids got sick and they came home early to find that someone had been here in their garage'

'Did they break in? Donald asked.

Constable Brooks shook his head. 'No, sir. No sign of a break-in and Mrs Moss is quite certain that nothing's been taken. There's been some paint spilled over the floor in there, and that's about it.'

Inside the garage Hodgkiss noticed a pair of blue jeans hanging on a nail in the wall nearby. 'Constable, do you know if there's a belt missing from those jeans?'

Constable Brooks turned to Hodgkiss, obviously unimpressed at being questioned by an elderly civilian. 'I've already asked Mrs Moss if anything's missing and she said not.'

Hodgkiss pressed. 'No doubt, constable, nevertheless would you mind asking her again, in particular about the belt?'

Constable Brooks turned to Donald for confirmation of the request.

Donald nodded. 'Might be worthwhile asking, constable,' he said.

Constable Brooke disappeared into the house and moments later the tip-tap of impatient high heels on tiles could be heard approaching.

Hodgkiss estimated Mrs Moss's age at more than forty summers.

A trim, hard-eyed blonde, she was not about to waste her valuable time satisfying the curiosity of a superannuee. 'I've already told the constable that nothing's been taken from here,' she said shortly. 'What's the problem now?'

Hodgkiss indicated the jeans. 'Is there a belt missing from the jeans?'

Mrs Moss glanced at the jeans. 'Yes,' she replied tartly. 'It had a wide brown leather belt with a silver buckle. Is that all?'

Hodgkiss nodded graciously. 'Thank you. And where do you keep the remote for the garage door?'

'There's one in each of the cars.' Mrs Moss snapped. 'Why do you want to know?'

Hodgkiss ignored the question. 'And were the car keys on the key ring you left with your neighbour?'

'No, of course not. Whyever would I do that?' said Mrs Moss. She turned and tip-tapped quickly inside.

'Neither co-operative nor observant.' Hodgkiss announced in tones loud enough to reach the retreating figure.

'Yeah, but why ask about the car keys ... and the garage door remote?' said Donald. 'Anyway, these sorts of doors can be opened without the remote if you're inside.'

Hodgkiss nodded. 'I realise that, Donald. I was just wishing to explore the possibility that Rolf Evers might have used one of these vehicles when he removed Whitten's body from this garage.'

'Assuming it was him that moved it and assuming it was ever in this garage in the first place,' said Donald, unwilling to concede a point to his father-in-law.

'Well there's one way to find out,' said Hodgkiss. 'Let's go and ask him. His car's out the front so he's probably at home.'

Rolf Evers was at home and not at all pleased to see who was waiting on his doorstep when he answered the knocker.

'Good morning, Mr Evers,' said Donald, in his best formal tone and displaying his identification. 'I wish to speak to you in connecting with the death and disappearance of Adrian Whitten whom I'm sure you have heard of, possibly through your sister.'

Rolf nodded. 'Oh, yes. 'I've heard about Whitten all right. A real bastard of a bloke according to Janice.'

'Do you mind if we come in?' said Donald as he marched into the hall, followed by Jan and Hodgkiss.

'And what makes you think that I know anything about what happened to him?' Rolf said, leading the way into a well-furnished lounge room just to the right off the hallway.

'Really, Mr Evers, you must think the police are complete fools,' said Hodgkiss. 'Tell me, did you or did you not attempt to collect the prize which the group at the IT Unit won'

For a moment Rolf Evers stood stunned. 'Who says I did?'

'The young woman who works at the news agency near

the Unit's office, that's who. The place you went to try to collect the winnings.'

'That's nonsense. The woman must have been mistaken,' Rolf said unconvincingly.

'I don't think so,' said Hodgkiss. 'She gave an excellent description of you, right down to the cast in your eye. Of course if you think she was mistaken we could go back there now so she could provide the police with a positive identification. Do you agree to that?'

'I'm not agreeing to anything,' said Rolf aggressively. 'And I want all you people out of my house ... now.'

Hodgkiss moved quickly. He stooped, seized Rolf by the right ankle and with a swift jerk upended him onto a three-seater lounge. He held the right foot up and examined the sole of the shoe.

'Would you like to explain how you got this paint on the sole of your shoe? White and grey paint. The same colours as the tins knocked over in the garage next door.'

Rolf wriggled ineffectually. 'This is assault,' he muttered.

Donald examined the shoe briefly then wrenched it off. He seized Rolf's left leg and removed the left shoe.

'I think you'd better come down to the newsagent's and let that girl have another look at you,' he told Rolf.

'But I haven't got any shoes to wear,' Rolf protested.

'You must have something to put on your feet,' said Donald. 'Slippers, thongs, sandals ... anything. Or you can come in your bare feet if necessary.'

Rolf retired hastily to his bedroom and returned wearing a pair of tartan slippers.

'Are you arresting me" he inquired tentatively.

Donald shook his head. 'No. At the moment you're just assisting us with our inquiries.'

'I promise you I didn't have anything to do with him being injured or shot or whatever happened to him.' He hesitated. 'When I first saw him I thought he must have banged his head because he seemed to be in a bit of a daze and there was blood on the side of his head.'

'And where was he when you saw him in this daze?' Hodgkiss asked.

'He was just standing in the driveway that runs down the side of their office building. He'd just come out of the side door from his office.'

Donald asked. 'Was he carrying anything when you first saw him?'

Yes, he was. Actually he had a gun in his hand.'

'And what did he do with it?'

'He didn't get a chance to do anything with it. I took it away from him, of course. You couldn't have him wandering around the streets in a daze with a gun in his hand. Later on I gave it back to him. I just put it in his pocket.'

'So what did you do when you found him standing in the driveway?'

'I took him over the road to my car.'

'And he went quietly along with you, did he … just like that?'

'Yes, he did. I swear. As I said before, he seemed to be in a bit of a daze.'

'OK, you took him to your car. What did you do then?'

'I told him I'd come to take him to a meeting and he came along quiet as a lamb.'

'And what were you doing there near the Unit in the first place?'

'I'd come to see my sister, of course.'

'Had you really?' said Hodgkiss sceptically. 'I don't believe that for one minute. You'd come there specifically to lay in wait for Whitten in the hope of stealing that winning lottery ticket that your sister had told you about. There's no point in denying it, Evers, because we know you had it in your possession. So let's not waste any more time.'

Rolf nodded. 'OK, then. I'd been hoping to run into him so I could take the ticket off him somehow. He had no right to be holding out on the others the way did. Anyway, I took him to the car and laid him on the back seat. I put down a piece of newspaper on the seat because I didn't want to get blood all over the upholstery.'

'And what did he do? Didn't he say anything? Didn't he want to know where you were taking him?'

Rolf shook his head. 'No. Most of the time he just lay there with his eyes closed. I had a look at him from time to time to see how he was. His pulse seemed all right and his breathing was quite OK. He didn't seem to think there was anything odd about me saying I was taking him to a meeting.'

'I suppose it never crossed your mind that he might be in urgent need of medical attention,' said Hodgkiss.

'No. He looked OK to me. As I said, he was a bit dazed but his breathing and pulse were fine.

'I had no idea then that he'd been shot. I thought he might have just knocked his head or something.'

'And didn't he ever ask anything about this meeting you said you were taking him to; where it was, who it was with or what it was about?'

Rolf shook his head. 'No. He never seemed to quite know what was going on around him. I just told him I was there to drive him and he seemed to think that was perfectly normal. So off we went. Later, when we were parked out in the national park, I took the ticket from his wallet.'

'But surely he must have wondered why he was out in the bush when he was expecting to go to a meeting. Didn't he say anything? Didn't he ask what you were doing there?'

Evers shook his head. 'No. By then he was passed out most of the time. He just wasn't registering anything.'

Donald sighed. 'All right. Get on with it.' What happened next?'

'After I got the ticket I realised I couldn't risk having him get his act together and start making waves before I'd been able to collect on the ticket, so I decided to drive home and then work out what to do with him.

'Then I remembered about Janice having the key to the Moss's place next door. So I drove home, got the keys, backed up and parked in their car port, opened their garage door and I put him in.'

'And tied him up with a leather belt,' put in Hodgkiss.

'Well, I had to, didn't I. I couldn't risk him coming to his senses, getting out and roaming around the place in the condition he was in. Besides he might have noticed that the ticket was gone and started to make problems. So I drove straight to the newsagent and tried to collect the winnings.

'That's when things began to go wrong. I found out that I had to fill in some form and even when I'd done that I wouldn't just get paid. They'd post out a cheque made out to Whitten because it was all in his name.

'So I knew I'd have to keep him under wraps until some-how I could sort things out with the lotteries people and actually get the money. I thought it'd be OK to just leave him there in the garage for a day or two. He seemed OK. But when I went back there the last time I realised he was dead. I've got to tell you that was a real shock … a real shock. So I backed the car up, put him in and took him out to the national park again and left him there. I mean, what else could I do? No point taking him to the hospital then. It was all a bit late for that. Of course I was very sorry about him dying, but what else could I have done. But I swear I didn't kill him.'

Hodgkiss demanded angrily. 'You kept him tied up with a leather belt for days without food or water! How do you know that isn't what killed him?'

Rolf protested. 'No, it wasn't that. I'm sure it must've been the wound on the head that did for him in the end. And I reckon when they do a post mortem that'll prove I'm not responsible. I never did anything to hurt him so how can I have killed him. Besides, he never asked for anything to eat or drink. Not once. He just seemed to be dozing most of the time. Quite peaceful he was.'

Donald put the two shoes in a large plastic bag produced from his jacket pocket. 'We'll see about that. Now I want you to accompany me to the police station where you're going to be charged with abduction or kidnapping or causing death by neglect ... or something along those lines.'

'But that's nonsense,' Rolf protested. 'I never kidnapped anyone. Whitten came along quite willingly.'

'But you said yourself he was in a dazed state. He should have been taken straight to the nearest hospital. And then there's theft of the lottery ticket. I suggest you ring your solicitor. Now, is your sister at home?' Donald asked. 'We need to have a word with her, too.'

Rolf shook his head. 'I don't know when she's likely to get home these days. Probably she's gone straight to the boyfriend's place. She often does after work and doesn't get home until next morning.'

Donald nodded. 'I see. Well, we'll catch up with her later.

Meanwhile I want a detailed statement from you; everything you said, thought or saw. OK?'

Rolf nodded miserably.

*   *   *

Next morning Donald and Hodgkiss arrived early at the IT Unit. Jan was already there with Eric Furlough and Janice Evers. David Caton had just been dispatched to the nearby shops for a carton of milk.

'I really don't think we can tell you much more than we told you before,' said Janice. 'Of course we know now that Adrian's body has been found out in the national park but we've no idea how he got there.'

'What we're particularly interested in at the moment, Ms Evers,' said Donald, 'is your actions here during the period immediately before you heard the shot.'

'Yes, we rather thought you might be,' said Furlough. 'So in order to assist you with your inquires, as the saying goes, we've found the relevant disc.'

He continued. 'None of us dared to turn the CCTV off after Adrian set it going again so the period you're so interested in is all on record.'

He turned to the computer on his desk and jabbed the keys. 'The half hour before the shot, you say. Just a moment.' Again his fingers played over the keys. 'Here you are. Ready to go.'

The others gathered around Furlough's desk and he put a finger on the mouse.

At once the screen came to life with a picture of the room where they were standing. Furlough and Janice were working at their word processors. Occasionally one would turn to the other to make a comment, but because the CCTV do not have sound nothing was heard.

'Nothing happens for about twenty minutes,' said Furlough. 'Do you want me to fast forward?'

'If you wouldn't mind,' said Donald.

Furlough struck a key several times and the picture changed in jerks. Then he pressed the Play key.

He said. 'This is where Janice asked David to go to the shop.'

On the screen Janice turned in her chair to face David who was standing taking something from a cupboard. David turned and crossed to where Janice was seated. She handed something to him and David headed for the door and disappeared off the screen.

The other two continued working. Several minutes passed.

Then abruptly they both looked up sharply.

'That was then we heard the shot,' Janice explained.

On the screen they both rose quickly from their chairs and hurried over to the edge of the screen where Furlough could be seen trying to open the door to Whitten's office then knocking vigourously on it. He leaned forward, lips moving.

'I called out a few times,' Furlough said, 'but there was no reply.'

On the screen Furlough dropped to a knee, eye level with the keyhole.

'As you know, inspector, the key was in the keyhole so I couldn't see into the room,' he commented. 'We knew there was no point going around to try to get in through the other door because it was always locked. The window too. So Janice rang triple zero and was put through to the police at

Crestwood. I think she was put through to you, Inspector Burke,' said Furlough.

Donald nodded. 'That's right. Now, I'd like to watch the rest of the CCTV up to the point when I arrive and break into the room, OK?'

'Certainly,' said Furlough. 'Nothing much happens except David comes back from the shops, but that was later. Meanwhile, we just hung around, trying to work, until you arrive. While you're watching may I get you a cup of coffee?'

Hodgkiss and Jan accepted the offer while Donald remained glued to the screen. For most of the time he saw Janice and Furlough talking animatedly or working at their computers, sometimes rising to hurry over to Whitten's door to knock or listen.

After about ten minutes Donald saw his own image enter the office through the back door and began a conversation with both Janice and Furlough.

'I think I've seen enough,' said Donald pushing back from the computer. 'Now there are one or two questions I'd like to ask the two of you about certain things you did a week or so before the shooting; things we saw on an earlier disc from your CCTV.'

'Certainly, Inspector,' said Furlough. 'Anything in particular?'

'Yes. The occasion we're interested in is when you entered Whitten's room carrying a loop of white-coated electrician's cable over your shoulder and some tools in your hand. Do you remember that?'

'I certainly do. What would you like to know?'

'We'd like to know what you were doing in Whitten's office. When you came out you seemed to be carrying considerably less cable. Would that be right?'

'Yes, that'd be right.'

'So what did you use the cable for?'

'I ran it from a power point up into the roof and along to the region of the external door. Then I lowered it down the cavity wall. The whole job took about an hour, I'd say.'

'But what was the job?'

'It was a special job Whitten wanted done. If you'd known him you would have soon realised that he had a thing about security. You must remember when you arrived we tried to get in to see if we could save him. But we couldn't get in, right? You had to break down the door. It wasn't just locked, it was bolted on the inside.'

'Yeah. I remember,' said Donald.

'Well, the job he wanted me to do in his room was to fit a bolt on the other door, the door that opens out to the driveway. But he wanted me to do it so he could lock and bolt the door from the *outside … after he'd gone out.*'

'That was a pretty extraordinary measure, wasn't it?' said Jan.

'An extraordinary measure for any normal person to take, but not Adrian,' said Furlough. 'And I wasn't about to argue with him. He even told me how to do it; with an iron bolt and an electromagnet. He gave me the money from petty cash to buy whatever I needed to get the job done.'

Hodgkiss asked. 'I take it you operated the bolt with a small device that looks like a garage door remote. Is that so?'

Furlough nodded. 'Yes, that's right. I've got one here,' he said, opening a drawer in his desk and taking out one of the remotes. 'You press the toggle this way and it turns the magnet on and push it the other way and it's off.'

'But that means he wouldn't be able to open the external door once it had been bolted? If he'd locked and bolted the door to your office he'd never be able to get back into his room.'

Furlough shook his head. 'But that's the point: he could open it even if he'd bolted it earlier because he'd dreamed up this idea of how to get back in even if the bolt was closed. It was really quite ingenious. He got me to fix a light coil spring around the bolt. The spring wasn't strong enough to stop the magnet pulling the bolt over into place, but when the current was turned off the spring pulled the bolt back so you could open the door. That way he could get back into his room if the door to our office was bolted, which it always was to stop us snooping. Not that there was anything to snoop for. He was obsessive about security.'

'And how many of these remotes are there?' Hodgkiss asked.

'Only two that I know of. This one,' he said hold up the remote, 'and the one I gave Whitten.'

'And where did he normally keep his remote?'

'I've really no idea,' said Furlough. 'I guess he took it home with him in his brief case.'

'Have you looked in his desk?' Hodgkiss asked.

Donald said: 'No need. It's not there.'

'Do you want anything more from us,' asked Furlough as David Caton came in the back door with a carton of milk.

'Not, I think that's all for the present,' said Donald.

*   *   *

'Well,' said Donald, 'I'd say we're back to square one.'

Donald, Hodgkiss and Jan were sitting in the unmarked police car parked in the road outside the Unit.

'It's a real muddle,' said Donald. 'Even if we find out who

shot him it doesn't follow that person's necessarily the murderer because we still don't know if he died from the shot in the head or from exposure after lying around in the Moss's garage for days.'

Hodgkiss said; 'I think we have reached the point in this inquiry where it may prove profitable to ask the question: *qui bono* — who benefits?'

'Well neither of those two benefit,' said Jan. 'They knew that I intended to close the Unit down for lack of work and bring them all back to head office. They lead an idyllic existence down here, except, of course, for Whitten. They have just enough work to keep them busy but not frantic. Good rates of pay. And both Janice and Eric Furlough knew that if Whitten left for some reason there would be no question of either of them being promoted to his job because the job would disappear when they were brought back to head office. They know that. I've told them both.'

'Then it looks like no one benefits?' said Donald.

'I think you're jumping the gun there,' said Jan. 'Don't forget that Whitten was threatening to post certain intimate photos on the internet.'

Donald nodded. 'Yes. I'd forgotten about that. There's no doubt that Janice at least had a motive although her husband doesn't seem particularly stressed about the situation, assuming he's aware of it.'

'Didn't Whitten have a sister?' Hodgkiss asked.

'Yes, he did,' said Jan. 'And it's generally believed that he treated her like dirt. He'd made a domestic drudge of her because she had no money, or rather because he had control of her money under the terms of their parents' will.'

'Well, *she'd* certainly have a motive,' said Donald. 'She

lives … lived with him, didn't she? I think we should pay her a visit.'

Donald was about to start the car when he saw Janice running up the driveway, waving her arms to catch his attention.

She arrived, breathless, mobile phone in one hand. 'I've got my husband on the phone. He rang to say he'd just thought of something that might be of interest. I think you should hear it.' She passed the phone through the window to Donald.

'Yes, Mr Evers,' said Donald. 'Your wife tells me you may have remembered something of interest about Whitten's death.'

'Yes,' said Rolf. 'It may be important or it may not. I just remembered that when I was sitting in the coffee shop opposite the Unit waiting to see if Whitten would come out, a rather odd thing happened.

'The waitress had just delivered my coffee and I had just thanked her, then when I turned back to look out there was a woman, I think it was Mrs Rainer, walking rather unsteadily across the road towards my car.

'When she was a short distance away she took out her remote and used it, pointing it directly at my car.

'Obviously she'd mistaken my car for hers because when she used the remote the car in front of mine flashed its lights.

'She seemed surprised and changed direction and went to her car which was exactly the same make and colour as mine.

'I couldn't say for sure that she'd come from the Unit but she'd certainly crossed the road from somewhere *near* the Unit.'

'Thank you, Mr Evers. You say it was Mrs Rainer. So you'd know her if you saw her again.'

'Yes, and I'd certainly know her car.'

Hodgkiss, who had been listening from the back seat,

leaned forward and called. 'Mrs Evers, what make of car does Mr Whitten's sister drive? And what colour is it?

'It's an early model Zeeta, beige,' she replied, then added: 'There aren't many of them around. They were total lemons.' She stood back from the car and waved. 'Happy hunting,' she called as the car drew away.

*   *   *

'I suppose you know the address for Whitten and his sister?' Hodgkiss asked as Donald steered the unmarked police car through the backstreets of West Lillimoor towards the Northern Highway.

'I've rung my P.A.' said Jan. 'She'll have the address for us in a minute.'

It was little more than a minute before Jan's mobile rang deep in her shoulder bag. She hunted it out and listened. 'Thanks, Jenny,' she said and turned to Donald. 'It's number eleven Cross Street. I assume his sister still lives there,' Jan said, returning her phone to the bag. 'Do you know where Cross Street is, Donald?'

'Sure do,' said Donald, turning on the left turn indicator. 'It's only a few minutes from here.'

The late Adrian Whitten had lived with his sister on the ground floor of an old-fashion block of flats.

Minutes later Donald pulled the police car to the kerb in Cross Street and parked the car behind an early model beige Zeeta sedan.

'Looks like she's home,' Jan commented.

According to a handwritten list in a glazed frame just inside the door to the entry lobby, Whitten occupied Flat one.

On the right side of the entry lobby was a dark stained door with a tarnished brass *One* screwed to the panel. The three gathered in a group in front of the door and Donald pressed the button in a small plastic fitting fixed, slightly crooked, to the wall to the right of the door.

They did not have long to wait.

The door was pulled open by a woman whom Hodgkiss decided would never see forty again.

In her hand was a half-full flute of champagne, held at an alarming angle.

'If you're looking for the charming Adrian you're too bloody late,' she announced tipsily. 'Someone did the world a favour and shot the bastard. But you know that, don't you?' she said pointing an accusing finger at Donald, 'because you're a copper, right?'

'Ms Sarah Rainer, is it?' Donald inquired dead-pan.

'Might be.' she slurred.

Donald reached into his jacket pocket and took out his identification folder. 'I want to talk to you about your brother … how he died, and what you can tell me about it. May we come in?'

'Sure, why not.' She glanced at Jan. 'I know who that lady is, but I don't know the old guy.'

'My name's Edgar Hodgkiss, Ms Rainer. I'm assisting Inspector Burke with this inquiry,' Hodgkiss said as he followed the others down a central hall to a kitchen at the rear of the flat.

'Champagne anyone?' Sarah invited, waving a half-full bottle at them.

'No, thank you Ms Rainer,' said Donald, 'and I would appreciate it if you would stop drinking long enough to answer a few questions.'

'Stop drinking! Not on your life. I've probably only got time for another glass or two.'

'And why is that?' Donald asked.

'Because you've come to take me away to gaol. Isn't that right, osifer?'

Donald avoided the question. 'Would you like to tell me where you were on the afternoon your brother was shot?'

She hiccupped. 'Don't remember.'

'We have a witness who saw your car parked opposite the IT Unit that afternoon. Do you remember driving there?'

Sarah shook her head and topped up her champagne, pouring more onto the slate floor than into the flute. 'Nope. Don't remember a thing.'

'The same witness says he saw you crossing the road from the direction of the Unit and that you tried to open his car with your remote. Do you remember that?'

Sarah burst into smiles. 'Yeah. Now I remember. I thought it was my car. It was 'xactly the same, but mine was parked just in front.'

'So you remember being at the Unit that afternoon?'

'Yesh. Now I remember.'

'Do you remember seeing your brother in his room just before you came out to the car?'

Hodgkiss was wearied of the formalities and the fencing.

He stepped forward, elbowing Donald to one side. 'Ms Rainer. Please may we stop playing games. You went to the Unit with a small pistol. You knocked on the side door from the driveway and your brother let you in. You shot him once in the head and when he collapsed you placed the pistol in his hand. You then made sure that the door to the inner office was locked and bolted then you left the way you came in. After you left you activated the remote that locks the bolt on the side door, leaving the room locked up tight.

'By doing that you hoped that the police, finding the body in a locked room, would assume that your brother had taken his own life. Isn't that true?'

Sarah hiccupped again. 'One hundred pershent shpot on, except for the bit about shooting him in the head. I would have liked to.' She lurched against the kitchen bench and spilled a cascade of champagne from her flute down the front of her dress. 'It's why I went there ... But no guts,' she said in a voice of true regret. 'No guts.'

Donald said. 'So you agree that you went there with a gun, meaning to shoot him. Is that right?'

'Shpot on, constable.'

'Do you mind telling us where you obtained the pistol?'

'No. Not at all. Dad brought it home from the war ... the Korean War, I think it was. Could have been Vietnam though. Can't remember which. It's been kicking around the flat for ever. Dad said it's about as much use as a pop gun.'

'But you claim you didn't use it ... you left without shooting him?'

'S'right. No guts,' she repeated mournfully. 'You know what the bastard did. He took the gun off me before I could shoot him. Took it away from me like he's always taken everything away from me my whole life. Then he abused me and punched me in the head and nearly knocked me out.'

Donald asked. 'Then when he'd taken the gun what did you do then?'

'He kicked me out ... gave me the bum's rush out the side door. But I gave him a piece of my mind before I left.'

'And what did you do when you were outside?'

'Nothing much. I tottered up the drive ... I was still woozy from the punch in the head ... crossed the road and nearly got in the wrong car. But I finally made it home.'

'Are you prepared to come to the police station now and make a statement to that effect?'

'Not 'till I've finished this,' said Sarah, holding up the champagne bottle which by now was empty.

*   *   *

Hodgkiss had just turned off the large television set in the lounge after the late news when Donald arrived home.

Hodgkiss rose to greet Donald at the hall door. 'I'd say from the look on your face that you didn't manage to persuade Mrs Rainer to change her story and confess.'

Donald collapsed into a wingback armchair opposite the television. 'Not a chance. Particularly after her solicitor arrived. And after she'd sobered up a bit.' He sighed. 'This time it's really back to square one.'

'Don't despair, Donald,' said Hodgkiss resuming his seat on the sofa. 'Perhaps it's time to have another look at Janice Evers and Eric Furlough. They certainly had motive.'

'You mean Whitten's threat to put their picture on the internet? I don't know if that's a strong enough motive. I rather formed the impression that her husband couldn't give a toss what she gets up to. And of course Furlough's not married.'

'Granted. But what about the lottery ticket? I suppose it's just possible they might kill to get their hands on that,' Hodgkiss said, then shook his head. 'No. That's not good enough either. There must be something we've missed. Would you mind just running through once more everything that happened from the moment you arrived at the Unit after the phone call about the shot.'

Donald sighed. 'OK. But I don't know what good it'll do.

When I arrived there I drove down to the parking area at the rear and went straight inside. The two of them were there, in the office, waiting.

'What about the other one … David Caton?'

'He'd gone to the shops.'

Hodgkiss nodded. 'Go on.'

Donald continued. 'First I tried banging on Whitten's door and calling his name, but there was no answer. Then I tried to open it but it wouldn't budge. I looked in the keyhole but the key was in the lock.

'All this time Janice and her boyfriend were urging me to force it open. They reckoned that if Whitten had shot himself he might still be alive and we might be able to do something to save him.

'So I broke down the door.'

'And what did you do when you first went inside?'

'Well, it was a bit of a surprise when we saw that the room was empty. I looked around in case there was somewhere he could have hidden but there was absolutely nowhere; no cupboards, no chests, no curtains … nothing you could hide behind … nothing.

'Then I noticed the other door in the side wall, so I went over and had a look at that. But it was fitted with a Yale lock and a bolt near the top of the door and it was in place.'

'What about the window?' Hodgkiss asked. 'I suppose you examined that.'

'Of course. It had one of those butterfly catch arrangements that lock the two frames together and it was firmly locked.'

'Do you know when Caton returned from the shops?'

Donald frowned. 'I'm not sure exactly when, but it must have been pretty soon after I got there. I didn't waste much time getting the door down and I'm sure he wasn't there before then so he must have arrived back very soon after ... while the three of us were in Whitten's office looking around and wondering what the hell had happened to him.'

'Did you actually see Caton enter Whitten's office?'

Donald shook his head. 'No. I'd been searching Whitten's desk and happened to look around and saw him; he was standing near the door to the outer office and I think he was holding a carton of milk in his hands. I suppose he'd just come back from the shops. Quite frankly, Dad, I don't see that it matters.'

Hodgkiss nodded slowly. 'Oh it matters all right. You know what, Donald; I believe that finally I have the solution to your problem.'

'The hell you have,' said Donald eagerly. 'Let's hear it then.' He got up and sat beside Hodgkiss on the sofa.

Hodgkiss spoke quietly and without interruption for five minutes.

When he had finished Donald nodded. 'By God, Dad, you could just be right. With Rolf Evers' statement and the CCTV vision of the critical time we should be able to make out a strong case. Luckily the room's been locked up ever since we left it, so if the evidence is still there we'll find it.'

'You might also have a chat to Ms. Rainer seeing she was on the spot when things were happening.'

Donald nodded. 'Good idea, Dad. I'll have a talk to her before I see the others.'

He got to his feet. 'I don't think there's any need to get everyone out of bed. Tomorrow morning will be soon enough to pay them a visit. I reckon I'll sleep well tonight.'

*　　　*　　　*

Janice turned from her computer.

'David, would you mind popping out for a small carton of milk? There's some money in the drawer.' Then a thought occurred to her. 'What did you do with the carton you went to buy the day Adrian … went missing? Is it still in the fridge?'

David nodded. 'No. In all the excitement I left it out and it went off.' He hesitated. 'There's something I need to tell you about that day… both of you.'

Furlough turned from his screen. 'Is this going to be a confession about keeping the change from the milk?'

David shook his head. 'No. And it's not funny.'

He hesitated. The others were watching him, puzzled.

'What is it, David? It can't be that serious … not about a carton of milk.'

David lowered his eyes. 'It's not about the milk. I'm afraid it's not a very pretty story.'

'What on earth do you mean, David,' said Furlough. Concerned now, he stood up from his work-station and crossed the office to sit beside Janice.

'I suppose I'd better tell you all about it. Besides, the police will find out eventually anyway.'

'What have the police got to do with it?' Janice asked, impatient now. 'David you're making no sense.'

David said simply. 'I killed him. Whitten. I shot him.'

Janice laughed uneasily. 'Don't be ridiculous, David. You weren't even here when he was shot.'

'I was, you know. That morning, after you asked me to get the milk I went out, up the drive and as I was walking past his room I noticed the side door to his office was half-way open.

'I could hear a woman's voice sounding very angry. I looked in and I could hardly believe what I saw. Adrian's sister, Ms Rainer … I knew her because she'd been to a couple of our Christmas parties in the old days … she was standing beside his desk with her back to me. I could see she had a gun in her hand and it was pointed at him.

'I turned around and I was just going to run back to the office and call for you to come and help. I was pretty panicked and hadn't a clue what to do.

'But then I thought there might be shooting and it could get dangerous, so I decided not to involve the two of you.

'Ms Rainer was standing between Adrian and me so I don't think he saw me … not then anyway.

'All the time I could hear her talking to him quietly now, but there was a real angry sound in her voice.

'She was saying how badly he had always treated her and that she wasn't' going to put up with it any more and that she was going to shoot him.

'She said he'd ill-treated her for years like he'd ill-treated everyone around him. She particularly mentioned both of you.'

'And what did he say about that?' Janice asked.

David shook his head. 'I don't remember. I don't think he said anything. He just got up, walked around towards her cool as you like, took the gun out of her hand and put it down on his desk.

'Then she started to cry. And that's when he hit her really hard in the head with his fist. She staggered back and nearly bumped into me.

'She must have been pretty dazed because she hardly seemed to register what was going on.

'And that's when Adrian noticed me. Straight away he launched into me for sneaking into his office.

'While that was going on his sister sort of staggered over to the driveway door. She just stood there, sort of moaning and swaying and leaning against the doorframe.

'Adrian went over and pushed her out into the driveway, told her to go home and he'd talk to her later. Then he shut the door.

'I was really angry at seeing him hit his sister like that so I told him what I thought of him. I called him a bully and a coward and he should be ashamed of the way he treated his sister. Then he told me to go and clear out my desk straight away and not come back. That I was sacked.

'When he turned away I just picked up the gun off his desk and shot him in the head.

'He must have heard me behind him because he was just turning around as I pulled the trigger and the bullet went into the side of his head at a bit of an angle.

'Of course I was absolutely terrified. At first I couldn't believe what I'd done.

'But there he was, lying on the carpet with his eyes open and staring and blood already seeping out from under his head.

'I thought of unlocking our office door and asking you for help but decided it would be unfair to involve you, particularly since it would come out about the CCTV business and the lottery prize and the police would treat you two as the main suspects straight away.

'I knew you must have heard the shot and would want to come in to investigate so I had to act quickly.

'Then I had the idea that if his body was found in a room that was completely locked up then everyone would think that he must have shot himself.

'So I wiped my fingerprints off the gun and put it in his hand and arranged his fingers as naturally as I could and pressed them onto it.

'Then I realised that somehow I had to get out of the room but still leave both the doors locked and bolted.

'First I thought of going out the side door and shutting it after I'd gone but I wasn't sure that the arrangement you'd set up with the bolt would still work properly. I never really understood how it operated anyway.

I couldn't see Adrian's remote anywhere and I was worried that if it was taken away out of range the power might cut out and the spring would pull the bolt back and that would ruin everything because then it wouldn't look like suicide any more.'

Furlough shook his head. 'It doesn't work like that, David. Once you turn the magnet on it stays on until you turn it off.'

David shook his head. 'I didn't know that. I didn't even know where the remote was then, although I found it later just outside in the driveway. Adrian must have dropped it. I picked it up and brought it back later and put it in my desk.

'And of course all the time you were banging on the door and calling out. That was panicking me too because I was worried you might break in.'

'I must have stood there just frozen for a few minutes before I realised how I could do it ... get out and still leave the room locked up tight.'

'The window,' Janice whispered.

'Exactly,' said David.

'I undid the catch, raised the lower sill, climbed out and closed the window.

'But I knew that somehow I was going to have get back in there and locked it properly before the police discovered that it wasn't fastened. That would have ruined everything.

'I didn't know if you'd rung for the police yet so I hurried down to the shop, got the milk and ran back.

'I saw the police car in the parking area and came inside just as the officer was breaking down the door.

'You could have knocked me over with a feather when I realised that Whitten wasn't in his office ... that somehow he'd gone. I couldn't figure it out.

'Anyway, as soon as both of you and the policeman went into Whitten's office I sneaked in, went straight to the window, put the catch in place and pulled the curtains across.

'I knew it was a hell of a risk to take. If the policeman had seen me fiddling with the window catch ... well, it would have been very hard to explain. But I had to take the chance. Besides I could see the policeman was busy looking through Adrian's desk.'

Janice said: 'I hope you thought to wipe your fingerprints off the catch when you'd locked it. I suppose you must have put your hands on the sill too.'

'No time. I couldn't risk it. He could have looked up at any moment. I wanted to get out of there before he noticed me. If he'd seen me wiping my fingerprints off the catch ... how bad would that've looked?'

'I don't think we need to worry about it anyway,' said Furlough. 'The scene-of-crime experts have been there and I didn't see any of their fingerprint powder on the window or anywhere near it. In fact I don't think they treated it as a crime scene at all. I'd say you're in the clear, David.'

A loud knock on the back door startled them.

Detective Inspector Burke entered the room. Behind him was a scene-of-crime officer in white overalls.

'We won't take a minute of your time,' Donald announced. 'There's just one more thing I have to check.'

He pulled back the police tape that still festooned the door to Whitten's office, opened it and entered.

He turned to the white-clad officer: 'Charlie, I want you to check the catch on the window and the sill for prints. OK?'

Minutes later he reappeared. 'Mr Caton. Would you oblige the scientific officer with a set of your fingerprints, if you please?'

*   *   *

Hodgkiss was slumped in the director's chair on the back deck studying the chess problems from he weekend papers when he heard the sound of a car door slamming in the driveway.

He climbed out of the chair, pulled back the heavy sliding door to the family room and hurried through to the kitchen in time to see Donald taking a can of beer from the small bar fridge under the kitchen bench.

Esme held up a hand. 'Dad, for heaven's sake, give Donald a moment to catch his breath before you start with your questions. Go back out on the deck and he'll be there in a minute or two.

Hodgkiss retreated to the back deck and settled on one of the curved benches surrounding the redwood table.

He had not long to wait. Can of beer in hand Donald joined him.

'Well, I charged him, Caton ... attempted murder,' he said. 'The best we could do in the circumstances. We still haven't had a definite report on the cause of death. The doctor said the bullet didn't do much damage to vital parts of the brain. Only one hemisphere was affected. He reckoned any half-way decent defence lawyer could put up a case that the shot wouldn't have been fatal. Apparently there's a good deal of medical history on wounds like that.

'And did you find his prints on the window catch, as I ... we thought?' Hodgkiss asked.

Donald took a gulp from the can. 'On the catch, on the

wooden frame, on the window pane … everywhere. We even got a scrap of material from the slacks he was wearing that had caught on the bricks outside when he climbed out the window.' Another gulp. 'He tried to deny everything at first of course … even that he'd been in Whitten's office that day. He reckoned he could have left his prints on the window some other time until I reminded him how he'd told you and Jan about Whitten keeping both his doors locked and bolted and never letting anyone in. And he couldn't explain how come Rolf Evers saw him come up the driveway, go in the side door to Whitten's room then saw him coming up the driveway again five minutes later. He had to have climbed out of the side window. He couldn't have gone out the back way then up the side again because the door to the office was locked and bolted on the inside when I got there and broke it down.

'Besides, Sarah Rainer finally remembered seeing him there in the room while she was arguing with her brother.

'Then I asked him if it was the other two who had put him up to it.

'That really set him off. He got so worked up denying they had anything to do with it that he completely stopped denying he did it himself.

'That's when he opened up and told us every thing.'

Hodgkiss nodded approval. 'That was very good psychology, Donald … giving him the opportunity to move the blame onto his friends, knowing he would never do it, thus leaving himself exposed. Congratulations. And what about Rolf Evers? What have you done with him?'

'He's been charged with kidnapping and unlawful imprisonment.

'I'd've charged him with manslaughter for failing to get Whitten to a hospital and that's still on the cards.'

Hodgkiss nodded. 'Well, as a locked room murder it certainly had its points of interest.

'Oh, and one last thing. Who's going to collect on the lottery win?'

Hodgkiss and the Ten Dollar Note

'Stop worrying, she'll bloody sign. I'll see to that if it's the last thing I do.'

Aubrey Anstey did not feel the confidence he presented as he gave the assurance to the two men sitting around the tiny glass topped table in the back bar of the Travellers' Hotel.

'Well you'd better get a wriggle on,' said Karl Offner, a local builder known more for the number of developments he had built rather than for their aesthetics or the quality of their workmanship.

Bob Eastwood, the chief town planner for the Kanundda Council, made his contribution to the discussion. 'And don't forget; if you don't get your plans approved before the elections next month you can bet that the new council, which will almost certainly be full of wankers from the protest groups, won't turn a blind eye to certain, um, irregularities in your plans.'

He continued. 'They'll soon work out that going on the size of your land you're only entitled to five stories.

'But throw in those two blocks Aubrey's missus owns and you can double the height of your buildings.'

Carl Offner snapped. 'Yeah, we know all about that. So Aubrey, you've gotta have a very serious talk to her. If it's delayed until after the election we'll be toast.'

Anstey asked hopefully. 'But surely mnay of the present council could be re-elected couldn't they? It's possible, isn't it?'

'Yes, it's possible,' said Eastwood, 'but it would be dumb to take the risk if we don't have to. You don't need me to tell you that nothing's certain in politics.'

He paused. 'And another thing; I'm taking one helluva risk personally by recommending that council approve your plans. It's my name on the recommendation to the sub-committee and the longer this drags on the bigger the risk of someone working out that I fudged the figures. So long as the smart alecs in the action groups can't get a look at the details we're safe enough. But a new council is going to have a close look at it and do the sums. That's when the brown stuff will hit the fan. So it's now or never.'

Anstey asked hopefully: 'But once council's given the green light we're home and hosed, aren't we? There's no going back unless council wants to pay buckets in compensation.

'Don't count on it,' said Offner. 'Just get your act together, get the extra land so you can put it up to council next week. What's the problem anyway? Your wife's never jacked up on you before like this, has she?' So what's gone wrong this time?'

'It's her mother,' said Anstey. 'She's been talking to her … putting ideas in her head.'

'Ideas. What kind of ideas?' Offner asked.

'Oh, you know. The usual greenie nonsense. Sustainability. Global warming. Carbon footprints. All that bull-shit.'

'But what's that got to do with us building a few blocks of home units … nice places for nice folk to live in.'

'Her mother reckons it's over-development. And it's not only her mother that's blowing in her ear; there's a woman lives in the same block where we live, woman by the name of Pat Strong.'

Eastwood nodded. 'Yeah. I know a bit about Pat Strong. She's trouble. And worse still, she's friendly with that narky old bastard Edgar Hodgkiss.' He turned to Anstey. 'If the two of them start blowing in your wife's ear we're all in big trouble.'

Anstey asked: 'Hodgkiss. Isn't he the fellah who's always writing to the local rag bagging the council?'

'That's the one,' said Eastwood. 'The pair of them are trouble with a capital T. So hurry up and have a very serious talk to whats-her-name your wife … Amelia, isn't it?'

Anstey nodded glumly. 'Yeah, that's her … Amelia.'

'Yeah. I remember warning you at the time about getting married to a bit of young stuff. Might be good in the cot for a while but look at what's happened now.'

'Yeah, maybe. But she wasn't just a bit of young stuff. She was a bit of seriously rich young stuff.'

'Yeah, well, rich or not, mate, her money's no good to you if you can't get your hands on it when you need it.'

Anstey replied angrily. 'Don't worry, I'll get it. She'll sign. One way or another.'

*   *   *

People who knew Amelia Powderley sometimes thought that she was rather too pleased with herself.

Certainly she had reason — her blonde hair, her well-spaced blue eyes, her wide, cupid's bow mouth, her excellent proportions. At school the boys crowded around clamouring for her attention and approval, then later, at university all the young men crowded about vying for her favours. Few of them saw beyond her obvious charms.

However, in addition to these assets, Amelia also possessed a shrewd intelligence which often went undetected beneath the layers of her superficial attractions.

Amelia soon recognised that intelligence was not the quality most valued by her many male admirers. So she often amused herself by playing the role of the dumb blonde, a stereotype which she reluctantly admitted to herself that she fitted perfectly.

But when she finally accepted an offer of marriage — a decision opposed by both her parents and one which she now regretted — her husband soon discovered that his wife had a mind of her own.

The first manifestation of this was her refusal to adopt his name as hers. This pleased her parents who were proud of their unusual surname and of the history of their line which could be traced back to a particular baron who had served King Charles the First and suffered for it.

Her refusal to give up her maiden name was only one of several demonstrations of her determination to be her own person. This was something her husband had not foreseen and he soon decided that responsibility for this unexpected and unwelcome display of independence rested on the shoulders of her mother who made frequent visits during the day time when he was occupied elsewhere.

He sometimes complained to his men friends: 'She turns up any time of the night or day and she sits there yakking away filling the wife's head with all this sustainability and feminist rubbish.'

When Mr Powderley died unexpectedly a very considerable bequest went to his daughter. Here again her independence asserted itself. It was her money, she informed her husband, and she would decide *how* it would be spent or *if* it would be spent. There was one direction in which it would *not* be spent, she assured him, and that was to finance any of his many home unit development schemes.

Amelia Powderley was an enthusiastic supporter of the several vocal community groups who opposed the proliferation of high rise residential blocks throughout Kanundda. She was a generous supporter of these groups whose purpose it was to defeat what they saw as inappropriate developments, thus setting her in direct opposition to her husband and his closest associates.

As she sat now, before the dressing table mirror in the bedroom of her expensive Kylerbrin home, she wished that she had used her intelligence to better effect in her selection of a partner.

Her mother had warned her about Aubrey Anstey.

'A mean little mouth,' her mother had told her after she had brought him home for the first time.

'Oh, mother. It's not fair to damn the poor fellow over of the size of his mouth. That's nonsense. It's unfair.'

'And bad tempered, too,' her mother had pronounced.

'Bad tempered!' she had protested. 'What on earth makes you say he's bad tempered.'

Her mother had replied without hesitation. 'His eyebrows meet on the bridge of his nose.'

She had laughed. 'What nonsense.'

But she was not laughing now.

In the mirror she saw that the blood from her lip had congealed from where he had struck her and her cheek was still smarting from the hard blow from his open hand.

The front doorbell rang. It would be her mother.

She had rung her mother as soon as Aubrey had left the house for a meeting, probably with one of his developer cronies. She hurried downstairs and opened the front door. Her mother burst in and embraced her.

Minutes later, in the kitchen, with the teapot between them, her mother, Claudia Powderley, said: 'It must not happen again. You will have to get a court order to make him stay away.'

Amelia sighed. Of course her mother was right. She could not allow this to continue.

Her mother continued. 'I suppose it was over money again, was it?'

Amelia nodded. 'He wanted me to sign papers putting those two properties in Markham Road up for sale so one of his mates could buy them at a knock-down price and run up some more of their ghastly town houses. He said it was an excellent investment. We'd make millions.'

'Don't you dare sell,' her mother snapped. 'Those places belonged to your gran.'

'Don't worry, mum. I've no intention of selling either of them.'

'Why does he want to knock them down anyway? They're wonderful investments and besides, the market's not good for selling at the moment.'

'Oh, he knows all that, but he's made some arrangement with that crooked builder Karl Offner. Offner owns other places in Markham Road but my two houses are smack in the middle of his land. If he can't buy them he's left with two small sites. He needs my two blocks if he's going to make worthwhile money.'

'And how is Aubrey mixed up in this?'

'I assume he's promised them he'll persuade me to sell cheap and they'll cut him in on their profits.'

Just then the phone on the dressing table rang.

'You answer it please, mum,' said Amelia.

Claudia picked up the mobile phone and glanced at the caller's ID in the window. 'Yes, Pat,' she said, and listened. Then; 'Yes, Pat, she's here.' She passed the phone to Amelia. Claudia looked out of the bedroom window at the well-tended back garden and neatly clipped lawn while her daughter spoke.

'No, Pat, I don't think I'll make it to tennis this week. Give the girls my apologies. I should be back on deck next week. Yes, there is something we need to talk about but I don't want to talk about it now. I'll tell you about it tomorrow. I'll ring you in the morning. I promise.'

She cut the call and returned the phone to the dressing table. She said thoughtfully. 'She's a good friend, Pat Strong.'

Her mother nodded vigourously. 'Yes. She was awake-up to Aubrey from the start too, wasn't she?'

Amelia nodded thoughtfully. 'Yes. You're right. Pat never liked him ... either.'

'You have to see Marcus Blake first thing in the morning. He'll know how to go about getting an order against that ... that coward.'

Amelia sighed. It would not be pleasant having to face Aubrey in a court of law, but it had to be done.

*   *   *

'Hodgkiss, I'm worried about Amelia. I think something's happened to her. She seems to have disappeared.'

Pat was driving her big silver Mercedes through the back streets of Lillimoor, Hodgkiss beside her.

'Why, what's happened?' he asked.

'I rang her on Monday morning early to see if she wanted a lift to tennis today as usual, but she put me off.'

'Well that's hardly cause for alarm, surely.'

'Perhaps not, but I could tell from her tone of voice that something was the matter … and her mother was there and she's not usually there that early. And she promised me she'd ring yesterday morning but she never called.'

'She lives in the same block as you, doesn't she?'

'Yes. Two doors down. I've rung her and I've been down and banged on her door, but there was no answer. Then I rang her mother who lives only a few streets away and she hasn't heard from Amelia since Monday either.

'And she mentioned that Amelia was supposed to be going to a solicitor yesterday to start proceedings to take out a court order to keep Aubrey away from her because he'd attacked her again.'

Hodgkiss asked. 'You don't think she could have just gone away somewhere by herself; you know, to think things over.'

Pat shook her head. 'She'd never go away without telling her mother. And when she says she'll ring, she rings. She's very reliable with things like that. No, Hodgkiss. Something's happened to her and I'm worried. I don't suppose there'd be any use telling Donald, would there?'

Hodgkiss smiled grimly. 'You mean tell him that she's missing and ask him to have the missing persons officers start looking for her? No, that would be no use at all. You know as well as I what he'd say: she hasn't been missing for long enough. We'll need a bit more than what you've told me to convince him that something's really happened to her.'

'Well, there is something more,' said Pat. 'On Monday night I didn't sleep very well and I happened to wake up about two in the morning. I went to my ensuite to get a drink of water and while I was there I heard the sound of a garage door going up then moments later I saw a car drive slowly down the driveway at the side of our block. I'm sure it was Anstey's car and he was driving with no lights on.'

'If he didn't have any lights on how do you know it was his car,' Hodgkiss asked.

'It had to be his. There are only two garages that use that section of the driveway and the Fossdicks in unit seven don't have a car, so it must have been Anstey.'

'Or Amelia."

'Yes, I suppose so. But where would she be going in the middle of the night … with no lights on? Only to her mother. And her mother hasn't seen her.'

Pat turned the big car into one of the parking spots near the Rosbury tennis courts where the Lindfield Ladies' Tennis Club met weekly to play.

They climbed out, Pat took her tennis racquet from the back seat and they went to join the two other women waiting in the tiny shed beside the courts.

As they approached Pat called. 'Amelia can't make it today. So it's going to be singles and cut-throat.'

Emma Carter, a tall, well-made dark-haired woman, replied: 'Perhaps Edgar could play. I've got a spare racquet and he'd fit into my sandshoes. He's got the smallest feet I've ever seen on a man.'

'It's a sign of good breeding,' said Hodgkiss stiffly. 'However, I doubt if I'd be anywhere near up to your standard.

It would be most unfair if I played because I'd just be lead in the saddlebags of whoever was my partner.'

'All right. Then you can umpire for us,' said Beth Wilson, a tiny, energetic blonde.

So Hodgkiss mounted the umpire's chair to supervise play.

However when all disputed calls were resolved in Pat's favour, even when his calls were blatantly wrong, Hodgkiss was soon obliged to climb down and return to the shed.

After one cut-throat and two singles matches the women decided to have a break. In the shed they took out thermoses of hot coffee and bags of biscuits. Hodgkiss poured and handed the biscuits around.

'Well there's something he can do right, Pat,' commented Beth.

They had finished their coffee and were about to return to the court for a cut-throat game when a mobile phone sounded.

At once Beth scooped up her handbag opened it and pulled out her tiny blue phone.

As she did so a ten dollar note fluttered to the ground.

Hodgkiss stooped to pick it up and return it. He hesitated. There was writing on the note.

Someone had written in green a series of numbers and symbols.

He showed the note to Pat.

'What do you make of that?' he asked.

Pat glanced at the note and shook her head. 'Not a lot. Why?'

Meanwhile Beth had finished her call. She nodded towards the note Hodgkiss was holding. 'My son, Tom, brought that home with him yesterday morning. He'd been out for his early morning run and found it lying in the street.

He thought his luck had begun to change. Ten dollars is more than he gets in pocket money.'

Hodgkiss said: 'I think there is a little more to this than meets the eye.'

'Why do you say that, Edgar? I only ask because Tom seemed to think that it was some kind of call for help.'

'Then Tom is a very observant young man. He is quite correct. It is obviously a call from someone in distress.'

'But why? What makes you say that?'

Hodgkiss held up the note. 'Those symbols, the three full-stops, the three dashes and the three full-stops, or dots, as they are called in Morse Code, are the universal plea for help: Save Our Souls, or in Morse SOS.'

'But why? I mean, who's going to write that on a ten dollar note? And what about those numbers? What do they mean? Are they part of a code too?'

'They are not part of any code that I know,' said Hodgkiss. 'But they must mean something. No one is going to write an SOS followed by a row of meaningless numbers. Whoever wrote them must have had some purpose in mind.'

'But why write them in lipstick?' asked Emma. 'I'm pretty sure that's lipstick.'

Pat nodded agreement. 'Yes, it's lipstick all right. But why write on a ten dollar note in lipstick?'

'I think the answer to that is quite obvious,' said Hodgkiss. 'They had nothing else to write *with* and nothing else to write *on*.'

Emma turned to Pat, raised an eyebrow. 'This is the famous Edgar Hodgkiss you've told us about, making deductions before our very eyes.'

Hodgkiss ignored the remark. 'And I'd say it was written in haste or possibly in the dark.'

'Oh, why is that?' asked Pat.

'For one thing the lines of writing slope and the series of numbers had to go to a second line because the writer reached the edge of the note before concluding the sequence.'

'And what about the lipstick, Edgar? What do you conclude from that?' Emma asked. 'Or is that a little out of your line?'

Pat interceded. 'I think I can tell you a little about the lipstick. It is a very new line; *Gregarious Green*, it's called.'

'I think Amelia wore that colour at tennis last week, didn't she?' asked Beth.

Pat nodded. 'I think you're right, Beth. Actually, now you mention it, I was with Amelia when she bought it at that new shop at St James Village. It had just come in.'

Hodgkiss returned the note to Beth. 'Beth, I would like your son to show us exactly where he found the note. Could you arrange that please?'

'No need for that. I can show you. Actually he found it right outside number 34 Boston Street, Rosbury, which is only about half a kilometre from our house. I went back there with him in case someone living around there had dropped it and was out looking for it. We were going to make inquiries at some of the houses nearby but since it had been pretty windy during the night we decided that we'd probably be wasting our time and that it could have blown for miles before he found it.'

Hodgkiss nodded. 'Yes, it has been windy this week. Good kite flying weather. And the numbers written on it ... 33335 ... they don't mean anything to you?'

Beth shook her head. 'No. And Tom couldn't make anything of them either.'

Hodgkiss reached into his pocket and took out his wallet. He unzipped one of the pockets and took out a ten dollar note. 'Beth, do you think your son Tom would like a nice new ten dollar note with no mysterious writing on it in exchange for this defaced specimen?'

'I'm sure he would,' said Beth. 'He was worried that he might have trouble spending it at the shops.'

The exchange was made. When Beth held out the note Hodgkiss took it gingerly by the edged and slipped it into a plastic envelope taken from his slacks pocket.

Beth smiled. 'Ah, fingerprints. Sorry Edgar. I'm afraid you'll find mine and Tom's all over it.' She added with a smile. 'I suppose you could take our prints for exclusion, as they say on the detective programmes on TV.'

'That may not be necessary,' Hodgkiss replied seriously.

'Do you really know how to take fingerprints?' Emma asked.

'Of course,' Hodgkiss replied. 'There is no big mystery about it.'

'But what do you use for fingerprint powder?'

'Cocoa.'

'Cocoa!' Emma exclaimed. 'Does it work?'

'Admirably. We've done it before, haven't we, Pat?'

Pat nodded. 'Of course it's not as good as the real stuff but it does show up prints quite well.'

'And whose prints do you think you find on that note, apart from Tom's and mine.'

'I've no idea,' said Hodgkiss.

'I think we've got to try to persuade Edgar's son-in-law that it might be worthwhile doing the job for us,' said Pat. 'But first we've got to convince him that something needs to be done.'

''Yes, and that is never easy,' Hodgkiss added glumly.

*   *   *

'Dad, you have to be kidding me.'

Hodgkiss' fears that Donald would not be easily persuaded to test the banknote for fingerprints were soon vindicated.

He had raised the subject during dinner while the two were sitting opposite each other in the built-in- pine breakfast nook in the kitchen of the Burke's Lillimoor bungalow.

Donald continued, reasonably. 'I bet it turns out that the kid wrote on it himself with his mother's lipstick for a lark.'

Hodgkiss shook his head. 'Donald, you cannot seriously believe that. For a start very few young people these days know that Morse code exists and almost none would be aware of the symbols to be used in seeking assistance.'

'I don't agree with you there. I think there are quite a few folk who know what SOS stands for.'

'Very likely, Donald. But I suggest that very few young people would know the Morse code elements used to make the signal.'

'OK. Dad. Let's assume the kid didn't write it. What are you suggesting?'

'I am merely suggesting that you should examine the note for fingerprints.'

'OK. And what will that prove? It may be an offence to deface a banknote with lipstick, but I promise you I'm not about to waste the time of our busy forensics boys with a dumb exercise like that. Besides, even if the person that did it *is* on record we're not about to charge them.'

'I am not suggesting you should Donald.'

'Well alleluia for that.'

'Why I want you to test the note for fingerprints is to ascertain whether or not the person who wrote that appeal for help was Amelia Powderley.'

'And what on earth makes you think it was this Amelia

Powderley woman that wrote it?'

'Because Pat knows that she bought a lipstick of that particular bilious shade of green recently.'

'Yeah. Pat's friend and about ten thousand other women in this city.'

Hodgkiss shook his head. 'No, Donald. That is most unlikely since that particular shade is only very new on the market.'

'Oh, and how come you're suddenly such an expert on ladies' cosmetics?'

'Because Pat told me. She was with Amelia when she bought a lipstick of that shade and that's what they were told at the time.'

'OK. So if her prints are on the thing so what? What does that prove?'

'What it proves, Donald, is that Pat's fears that her friend Amelia has met with foul play are fully justified. She fears that this lady has been abducted by her husband who has assaulted her on numerous occasions in the past.

'In addition she had promised to ring Pat on Tuesday morning and when she failed to do so Pat went looking for her. She rang her home and she knocked on her door. She rang her mother who is concerned for the same reasons. Also Pat saw her husband's car leave their block of town houses on Monday night late in a furtive manner.'

'A furtive manner. How does a car behave in a furtive manner?'

'By not displaying any lights when being driven at night time.'

'So what you're telling me is that you think this friend of Pat's has disappeared. Right?'

'Yes, Donald. Precisely.'

'OK then. You know the drill: when a missing persons report is made a squad of trained officers with years of experience in looking for missing persons will swing into action and look for her ... if she hasn't come home by then.'

During this conversation Esme, Donald's wife of nearly thirty years, had been packing the dishwasher under the bench near the sink. She closed the door of the machine, set in to its regular cycle, took off her apron and slid into the narrow seat beside her father.

'I've been listening to what Dad's been saying, Donald, and I think it wouldn't hurt just to have the note tested, would it? It wouldn't be a very big job for your scientific people, would it?'

'That's not the point,' Donald began.

Esme went on. 'I think Pat's a very level-headed woman. She's not the sort of person to start worrying about her friend for no good reason, is she?'

'No. but ...'

'And it is rather strange, isn't it, someone writing an SOS on a ten dollar note. I mean, no one's going to do that unless they're really in trouble, are they?'

'No, perhaps not. But don't you see ...'

'Anyway, I'd like to see this note. Do you have it there, Dad?'

'I certainly do, my dear,' said Hodgkiss, appreciating his daughter's support. He reached into his shirt pocket for the clear plastic envelope and handed it to Esme.

She scrutinised it through the envelope. 'It's an SOS all right,' she confirmed. 'We learned that much about Morse code at school. Have you any idea what the numbers mean, Dad?'

Hodgkiss shook his head. 'No. Not yet. But I intend to find out.' He paused then continued. 'I rather fear that discovering the meaning of those numbers is going to be our greatest challenge.'

'And you know where the note was found?'

'Yes. In Boston Street, not far from the shops in the Rosbury Village. It was found yesterday morning lying in the street by the son of one of the women in Pat's tennis group. But it was windy on Monday night and there's no telling where it was released.'

Esme asked sharply. 'Released? Why do you say it was "released?"'

Hodgkiss shrugged. 'It's just an idea I had. I suppose it could have been simply dropped. But it must have been dropped with a purpose. It was meant to be found and it was intended, or should I say hoped, that who ever found it should recognise it as a cry for help.'

Donald groaned. 'Oh, no. please.'

'That's enough of that Donald,' said Esme. 'You know that Dad sometimes gets good ideas about this kind of thing.'

Donald nodded vigourously. 'Oh yeah. He gets good ideas all right. Too many dammed ideas. Well this is one idea too many; messages written on a bank note in lipstick. If I told the boys at the station about this one they'd laugh for a week.'

'So you don't believe it's an attempt to get help?' Esme asked.

'No, love I do not.'

'Then how do you explain it?' Hodgkiss demanded.

'I say it's some kid's idea of a practical joke, that's how I explain it.'

'What? With a ten dollar note?' said Esme. 'Some joke!'

'OK, then love. What about those numbers? Have you got the faintest clue about what they mean? They're just a random jumble of numbers. If they were an address or a phone number or something that meant anything to anyone then perhaps there'd be something to investigate. But until someone can tell me what those numbers mean … forget it.'

He slid out of the breakfast nook and headed for the hall. Moments later they heard gales of electronic laughter coming from the TV set in the family room.

Hodgkiss looked thoughtfully at the ten dollar note. 'It appears we will have to interpret the significance numbers if we are to have any assistance from the law,'

*　　*　　*

'Well, mate, did you persuade the little woman to sign on the dotted line yet?'

Bob Eastwood made this inquiry without any real hope of receiving the answer he wanted to hear.

He added: 'I ask because time is running out. The election is only weeks away now and the mayor's team has about as much chance of winning as a snowflake in hell.'

Aubrey Anstey, to whom the question was addressed, replied with a transparently empty attempt at bravado: 'Oh, don't worry, she'll sign all right. I really showed her I meant business the other night.'

'Oh yeah? So what did you do to her?' asked Karl Offner, with a flicker of hope.

'I gave her a little something to remember me by,' replied Anstey, brandishing a fist.

'You whacked her?' Offner asked, alarmed. 'Was that a good idea? They don't all respond well to being knocked around.'

'Yeah, but I didn't leave it at that?'

Eastwood asked, nervously: 'Why? What else did you do to her?'

'After I'd given her one I thought it best to go out for a little while to cool off and give her time to think about it.

'Then just as I was leaving her mother drove up.

'She must have been on the phone to her straight away so I thought I'd better go back and have a listen to what they were talking about … and a good thing too.

'First of all that Pat Strong woman rang her about their tennis club. She decided to give it a miss which isn't all that surprising since she wouldn't want her classy girl friends to see her with a fat lip.

'Then I heard her and her mother talking about a court order to stop me going into my own home. Can you believe that?'

'Yeah, I can believe it,' said Eastwood. 'So, what did you do then?'

'I waited until it was dark and I took her down stairs to the car park, put her in the back of my car and took her to a mates' place not far away.'

'I suppose she went quietly, did she?' Eastwood inquired sarcastically.

Aubrey shook his head. 'She threatened to scream the house down so I hit her …not hard, just enough to stun her while I put a piece of tape across her mouth to shut her up.'

'I told her I was going to take her out in the car for a ride.'

'I saw straight away that she thought I meant take her for a ride in the Mafia sense and that really shook her up.'

'I'm not surprised. You could have chosen your words better. So what happened?'

'I was just pushing her towards the door when she turned and pointed to her handbag. So I got that for her and led her down the fire escape to the car.'

'I hope you checked her mobile phone wasn't in the hand bag.'

'What do you think I am? A complete fool.?'

Eastwood raised an eyebrow but said nothing

'Anyway I drove to this mate's house and took her down into the basement. He gives me his keys when ever he goes away so I can use the place for … meetings.'

Offner sniggered. 'Yeah. And we know the sort of people you'd be meeting.'

Anstey continued: 'Anyway the fellow who built this place originally was a music nut and he built a complete sound proof recording studio in the basement. She could scream her lungs out there and no one'd be any the wiser.'

'That still doesn't get the papers sighed, does it?' said Eastwood.

'It shows her I mean business. I reckon she'd've got the message by now.'

Eastwood shook his head. 'Somehow I've got this nasty feeling that you underestimate that woman.'

*   *   *

'I was so glad when you rang,' said Mrs Claudia Powderley, as Pat and Hodgkiss took their seats on the three-seater lounge opposite her.

It was Hodgkiss' first visit *chez Powderley*. He was most impressed. In the living room, where they were sitting, was a baby grand piano with a volume of Grieg's Lyric Pieces open on the music stand. Against the walls was a scattering of very fine examples of small Georgian furniture and a portrait in oils of Amelia hung over the faux fireplace.

Mrs Powderley, following the direction of Hodgkiss' gaze, contributed; 'she was a very beautiful girl.'

'She still is,' Hodgkiss contributed.

'But she won't be for very much longer,' said Mrs Powderley. 'Worry and fear are two very aging emotions and my poor Amelia is both worried and fearful; very fearful of that brute of a husband and worried about what he might do to her. And I can't begin to tell you how worried I've been since she disappeared. I just don't know what to do.'

'Have you rung the police about her disappearance?' Hodgkiss asked, knowing what the answer would be.

Mrs Powderley nodded. 'Yes, I tried that but they said she hadn't been missing for long enough. The young fellow I spoke to even had the cheek to suggest that she might have gone off with some man. I soon put him right about that.'

Hodgkiss took the plastic envelope containing the ten dollar note from his pocket and handed it to Mrs Powderley.

'This was found lying on the roadway in Boston Street at Rosbury early on Tuesday morning. Pat and I think Amelia might have written it.'

Mrs Powderley examined the note. 'It's certainly her shade of lipstick. But of course the writing could be anyone's. There aren't any written words you could make a comparison with. Of course I know what SOS means and so did Amelia, I know that for a fact. There was a chapter on Morse code in a book she used to read as a little girl.'

'What about the numbers?' Pat asked. 'What do you think they mean.'

Mrs Powderley frowned. 'There aren't enough of them for a phone number, are there? I suppose it could be an address if whoever wrote it was in too much of a hurry to write it out properly.'

'But it couldn't possibly be an address,' Pat objected. 'There are too many numbers. I can't imagine any street anywhere around here long enough to have a house number 33335.'

Mrs Powderley shook her head. 'No, I didn't mean a number like that. But imagine if who ever wrote it was in such a hurry that they left out the important bits, like strokes and dashes.'

Pat frowned. 'I don't follow you.'

Mrs Powderley held up the note. 'Now, for instance if it was referring to a flat in a block of units it could be unit 3 in a block that was 33-35 in some street or other. That way you'd have an address like 3/33-35, wouldn't you?'

Pat nodded. 'You would indeed. That's certainly something worth thinking about. But meanwhile do you have any idea at all about what could have happened to Amelia?'

Mrs Powderley came back immediately. 'Oh I've no doubt in the world that her husband has taken her away somewhere and is holding her prisoner there. She would never have gone by herself without telling me.

'But why would he want to hold her prisoner?' Hodgkiss asked, incredulous.

'Oh, there's no mystery about that either. He's been trying for months to make her sign an agreement to sell two cottages she owns so that he and his developer friends can buy them and incorporate them in a site where they hope to build more of their jerry-built town houses.'

Pat nodded. 'I see. That makes sense. Have you any idea where he might have taken her?'

Mrs Powderley shook her head. 'No. And she can't even ring even if she had the chance because she left her phone at home. I brought it back here with me in case she tries to ring it.'

'That could be very useful, Mrs Powderley,' said Hodgkiss, 'because we could use it for a fingerprint comparison test with any prints on that ten dollar note.'

'But how could you possibly take the fingerprints. Surely only the police can do that and they're not the least bit interested in what's happened to her.'

'Taking fingerprints is no great mystery,' said Pat. 'Hodgkiss and I have done it before.'

Hodgkiss asked. 'Do you happen to have any cocoa powder in the house.'

Mrs Powderley smiled and asked brightly. 'Certainly. Would you like a cup?'

*　　*　　*

Donald examined the white A4 sheet with its two neatly attached rows of even sections of sticky tape, each containing in its centre a faint brown pattern.

He glanced up to where Hodgkiss and Pat Strong sat opposite him at the round redwood table on the back deck.

'And what on earth am I supposed to make of this mess?

Hodgkiss shook his head angrily. 'Donald, why must you turn every one of our productive endeavours into a confrontation? You know damned well what it is.'

'If you're telling me these blotches are finger prints then I have to tell you that they would be totally useless for comparison with anything on record and worse than useless in a court of law.'

'We never intended that they should go anywhere near a court of law. We made them merely to demonstrate to you that it was Amelia Powderley who wrote that SOS on the ten dollar note.'

'You can't possibly know that on the basis of these,' said Donald jabbing a scornful finger at the A4 sheet. 'Where did you get these in the first place?'

'We took them from her mobile phone which her mother very sensibly allowed us to test for prints. That's the top row. The second row are prints taken from the front and back of the ten dollar note.'

Donald shook his head. 'I suppose you're going to tell me that they match the prints from the mobile phone. Even if they do, don't you see, that still proves nothing. It certainly doesn't prove that Amelia Powderley wrote on that ten dollar note. Anyone could have done it. She could have received the note in change from a shop with the writing already on it. It's not unusual to get notes with writing on them.'

When Hodgkiss was about to protest Donald held up a hand. 'Yes, I know about the new colour lipstick. But again, Dad, it doesn't prove anything. Surely you can see it's totally unreasonable for me to arrange for our already stretched police resources to be diverted to look for this woman.'

'All I can see, Donald, is that, as usual, you are being willfully obstructive.'

Donald continued with an attempt at conciliation: 'If you could work out what that number means it might help. It might mean something that actually gives us a clue to what's going on … if anything.'

Pat decided to try to lower the temperature of the conversation. 'So what do *you* think happened, Donald? Do you have a theory about who wrote on that note and why?'

Donald shrugged. 'I'd say the most likely answer is that someone's having a practical joke. There are people who write messages and put them in a bottle then drop them in the water to see what happens.'

'Oh, so that's your idea is it, Donald?' Hodgkiss demanded angrily. 'Well all I can say is that I hope you're right and that an innocent woman is not suffering because of your lack of foresight and imagination.'

'Yes, I certainly hope so too,' said Donald rising. 'If it'll make you any happier I'll take these with me and show it to the boys in the fingerprint section and see what they've got to say. But don't hold your breath.'

Hodgkiss said peevishly: 'Donald, I had not intended you to show those prints to anyone since it is almost certain that they will not be on record. I took them only to demonstrate to you that it was Amelia Powderley who wrote on that note. Seeing you do not accept that, then further examination of them is pointless.'

Donald tossed the sheet back onto the table. 'Fine. Have it your way,' he said and disappeared through the sliding door to the family room.

'Now what? asked Pat.

'Obviously we must continue our efforts to unravel the mystery of those numbers. What did you think of Mrs Powderley's theory about the street number?'

Pat shook her head. 'I don't buy it for a moment, Hodgkiss, although I suppose we should at least try to find a unit that fits that address somewhere in the vicinity of Boston Street.'

Hodgkiss pushed back his bench and rose. 'Very well. Then let's get on with it. Your friend Amelia may be in urgent need of assistance as we speak.'

'I hope things aren't that bad,' said Pat, following Hodgkiss through the house towards the front door.

'So do I,' said Hodgkiss, 'but bearing in mind what we know about her husband and the demands he was making of her I would say that we have ample reason to fear that Amelia Powderley may be in serious trouble.'

Ten minutes later Pat was driving the Mercedes slowly through the back streets of Rosbury on the western side of the Northern Highway.

She pulled to the kerb. 'Well, Hodgkiss we've been up and down half the streets in Rosbury and the ones that had a number 33 in them were all just bungalows; typical houses for this area. Not a single block of units.'

Hodgkiss nodded. 'Yes. I think we're both very familiar with this area and I cannot think of a unit block within miles. I fear we're wasting our time and your petrol.'

Pat frowned. 'There's something about that string of numbers lurking at the back of my mind. I have a feeling that if I don't try too hard it'll come to the surface and we'll be in business.'

'Well I sincerely hope your right, Pat. Do you think it would help if we bought a nice bottle of Pinot Grigio and went back to your unit for a good hard think?'

Pat smiled. 'I know what your idea of a good hard think is code for, Hodgkiss.'

'So, does the thought depress you?' Hodgkiss said sliding a hand onto Pat's thigh.

'Not in the least.'

She made no attempt to remove the hand.

*   *   *

But the next day, around noon, when Pat drove Hodgkiss, home neither had managed to attach any meaning to the five numbers written tantalizingly in green lipstick on the ten dollar note that was still encased in the plastic envelope in Hodgkiss' shirt pocket.

'We're no further ahead,' Pat confessed to Esme. 'You'd think that by now one of us would have been able to come up with a bright idea, but … nothing.'

After morning tea Pat returned home to attend to a stack of ironing and Hodgkiss took the chess problem, clipped neatly from the weekend papers, with him to the back deck to seek a solution, while Esme drove away in the small family car a shopping trip to the Lillimoor village.

While Hodgkiss was pondering the chess problem and Esme was shopping busily at Lillimoor, Pat's morning had taken an unexpected turn.

The big Mercedes, Pat at the wheel, was waiting at the traffic lights near the Rosbury shops, the right trafficator winking.. When the lights the car moved off, turning right into Challis Street then just a few hundreds metres further on, it turned left into Boston street where it stopped.

After a few moments it started again moving slowly, pausing every fifty metres or so as if the driver was searching for a particular house number.

At last it stopped and Pat Strong stepped out and walked purposefully up the drive of one of the houses, number 30, on the high side of the road.

She rang the door bell and waited. Very soon a middle-aged woman, wearing a cheerful apron and her hands encased in dripping rubber gloves, opened the door.

'I'm sorry to trouble you,' said Pat, smiling, 'but I'm looking for a Mrs Powderley. I thought she lived next door but there doesn't appear to be anyone at home there.'

The woman shook her head. 'There's no one called Powderley lives next door. A Mr and Mrs Simmonds live there but they're away overseas at present.'

Pat nodded, disappointed. 'That's strange,' she said. 'I could have sworn I was told number 32.'

'You say you rang the bell and no one came?' the woman asked.

Pat nodded. She didn't enjoy telling lies.

'That's odd,' said the woman, 'because just now I was upstairs and I saw a man in the backyard of the Simmonds place. He was walking around talking on his phone and waving his arms in the air. Looked very agitated, he did.'

'Maybe I should try again,' said Pat.

'Yes, maybe you should. I know that sometimes when the Simmonds go away they let a friend stay in the house to give burglars the impression that someone lives there. Maybe that's what's happened.'

'Do you know if the person staying there arrived on Monday or Tuesday.'

The woman paused, thinking. 'I think they must have arrived on Monday night because their burglar alarm went off and woke me up.'

'Would that have been in the early hours of Tuesday morning?'

'Yes, I believe it was. I saw a strange car drive up and leave again next morning. You seem to know a lot about what's going on next door. I thought I might ring the police but decided not to since it's probably one of their friends who's staying there. I don't suppose you'd care to tell me just what's going on?'

'I think you'll find out soon enough,' said Pat, turning and heading back down the driveway 'Thanks for your help.'

*　　　*　　　*

Later that morning, when Hodgkiss and Esme were eating a lunch of cheese and tomato sandwiches in the breakfast nook Hodgkiss phone rang. He took it from his shirt pocket and examined the callers ID in the window.

'Yes, Pat,' he said. 'What news?'

As he listened his eyes widened in astonishment. 'Are you quite sure?' he asked. Then: 'Yes. I'll be waiting out the front.'

He cut the connection.

'What was that all about?' Esme asked anxiously.

'Pat thinks she knows what the numbers on that banknote mean.'

'Are you going to tell Donald?' Esme asked anxiously.'

'Yes, of course.'

'Are you going to tell him *now*? You know how he feels about you and Pat running off and doing things on your own without telling him first.'

'I assure you, Esme, there is absolutely no cause for concern. We are not children. We do not need Donald to approve our every action.'

'Yes, I've heard that before,' said Esme. 'And I can remember more than one occasion when ...'

'Esme. Enough,' Hodgkiss snapped. 'Pat will be here shortly.'

He slid out of the breakfast nook and hurried down the hall to his bedroom at the front of the house where he took his jacket from behind the door then went out to wait on the nature strip.

He had been waiting only minutes before the big Mercedes slid to the kerb. Hodgkiss climbed in and fastened his seat belt.

'Well, tell me ... what does the number tell us?'

Pat smiled. 'It tells us where that ten dollar note was

dropped and very probably where Amelia Powderley is right now.'

'A very clever ten dollar note,' said Hodgkiss. 'Now, tell me, if you would just how did an item of currency manage to impart so much valuable information?'

It took Pat less than a minute to explain.

'Very ingenious of you, my dear,' said Hodgkiss, smiling. 'Congratulations are in order. Have you attempted yet to verify your theory?'

Pat nodded. 'Yes. I made discrete inquiries at one of the neighbouring houses and learned of mysterious nocturnal vehicular movements and the fact that the owner of the house is at present overseas. That's why the neighbour remembered comings and going in the middle of the night. She was tempted to ring the police but decided not to because she knew that the owner occasionally allowed friends to use his house while he was away.'

Hodgkiss smiled. 'Sounds promising.'

In less than five minutes Pat edged the car to the kerb outside a large red brick house set well back from the road.'

'This is the place,' she said. 'Come and see.'

They both climbed out and walked along the road to the driveway which led through high wrought iron gates to a garage under the house.

At the point where the driveway crossed the footpath Pat stopped. She pointed upwards. Hodgkiss' eyes followed the finger. He nodded, smiling. 'Very clever of you, my dear. Full marks.'

'Thank you, Hodgkiss. It wasn't all that clever. Just a matter of waiting until my memory slipped into gear. The question now is what do we do next?' Pat asked. 'Any ideas?'

'There's only one thing we can do. Confront the man,

assuming he's at home. I would say without a shadow of doubt that he is a coward. That much is obvious from the way he treats his wife. And like all cowards he'll go to water at the first whiff of grapeshot.'

'Don't you think we should ring Donald and let him fire the grapeshot?'

Hodgkiss shook his head emphatically. 'No point in that. It'd be complete waste of time.'

Pat protested: 'But he said if we could work out what the numbers mean he'd take us seriously.'

'He still wouldn't accept that this is the place. No. We have to do this on our own. Now, I suggest that you wait in the car while I do a little investigation.'

Pat was horrified. 'No, Hodgkiss. Absolutely not. You are not going in there alone.'

'Pat, I promise you I will not create a confrontation. I will simply inquire if there is a Mrs Powderly living at that address and if he says no, as he surely will, I will turn around and come straight out again. I promise.'

'But if he says no and you just walk away then we'll be no further ahead, will we?'

Hodgkiss shook his head. 'I don't agree. I will be able to tell at once if he's lying from how he reacts when I ask about his wife.'

Pat frowned. 'I don't like it.'

'There's nothing to be concerned about. If I don't come back within, say, fifteen minutes, then by all means ring Donald.'

'But I don't have a number for him in the middle of the day.'

'Then ring Esme and she'll ring him for you. She has his police mobile number.'

Unwillingly Pat agreed and Hodgkiss pushed open the ornate wrought iron gates guarding the gravel driveway to the house and set off briskly up the drive.

Pat returned to the car and stood, leaning on a mudguard, watching Hodgkiss' rapidly receding figure. She saw him mount the steps to the front porch and use the knocker on the front door. He turned and waved, smiling broadly. She waved back nervously. She saw the door open and a man appeared in the doorway. She was too far away to hear the conversation that took place, but after very few words were exchanged the man stood to one side and Hodgkiss turned to glance in her direction before entering the house. The door closed behind him.

Pat opened the Mercedes door and slid into the driver's seat. She glanced at her watch.

Fifteen minutes he had said.

Nearly twenty minutes had passed when Pat saw the garage door at one side of the house begin to rise. She started the Mercedes motor and slid the selector into Drive.

A large black car emerged from the garage and the door began to descend.

Pat eased the Mercedes away from the kerb and turned sharply into the driveway of the house blocking the path of the oncoming vehicle.

The driver stopped his car inches from the Mercedes' bumper bar. He opened the door and stepped out.

'What the hell do you think you're doing?' he called angrily. 'Kindly get that thing out of my driveway.'

Pat opened her driver's door and she too stepped out, but remained standing close beside the car.

'I will move out of your way as soon as you release Mr Hodgkiss and Amelia Powderley.'

For a moment the man was speechless. Then: 'I don't

know what you're talking about. I don't know anyone named Hodgkiss.'

'You do. Mr Hodgkiss is the gentleman who entered your house not twenty minutes ago. There is no point in denying it Mr Anstey. I was watching.'

'OK. Now move that car or I'll push it out of the way.'

'Then you should know that my car is in Park, the handbrake is on and it weighs at least two tons. If it's a test of horse power you want I'm quite confident that my Mercedes could push your car backup the drive to the garage where you came from.'

The two stood facing each other. Into this brief period of silence came the sound of a distant siren.

Pat seized quickly on this stroke of luck. 'And I should mention that I've already rung the police. They should be on their way here now.'

Anstey took one menacing step towards Pat, then stopped and turned abruptly and hurried back to his car.

He pulled open the back door and Hodgkiss tumbled out onto the lawn beside the driveway. His feet were bound together with tape at the ankles and his hands were bound at the wrists. A strip of tape covered his mouth. He kicked and struggled energetically on the grass like a large fish newly-landed on the deck of a trawler.

After him Amelia Powderley slid out of the back of the car, her mouth taped over and her hands taped together. She sat on the driveway, leaning against the side of the car. Anstey removed the tape binding Hodgkiss' hands and slid behind the wheel of his car and quickly locked all the doors.

Hodgkiss tore the tape from his mouth and began abusing Anstey with vigour and variety. Anstey revved the motor of his car to drown the words.

Then Hodgkiss tore the tape from his ankles, hurried to where Amelia sat, removed the tape from her wrists and mouth, helped her to her feet and they both hurried down the drive and climbed into the back of the Mercedes.

Pat slid the selector into Reverse.

As soon as the Mercedes had cleared the driveway Anstey drove into the street and accelerated away in the opposite direction.

But before it was out of sight Hodgkiss had made a mental note of the car's registration number.

Then with a mobile phone borrowed from Pat he rang Esme with a message to inform Donald of the number of the vehicle in which he and Amelia Powderley had been briefly imprisoned.

*　　*　　*

'I never thought for one moment that he'd actually murder me. He's much too cowardly to do anything like that.'

Amelia Powderley was giving an animated account of her trials at the hands of her husband to an audience consisting of Hodgkiss, Pat and Esme who were gathered in an attentive group around the Burke's round red wood table.

Hodgkiss nodded sympathetically. 'Just the same it can't have been much fun having your mouth taped over and being slung in the back of his car in the middle of the night.'

'No, it wasn't. But what I was mostly afraid of was that he might hand me over to one of his crooked friends who might think nothing of a spot of torture or even homicide.'

Esme asked. 'What gave you the idea of writing that message on the ten dollar note?'

'That was sheer desperation. I knew I had to try something

to leave a clue about where Aubrey was taking me. I knew he'd locked the car doors, then I remembered that he always leaves one of the rear windows in the car down just a fraction to let in fresh air, so I knew I could drop a message out if I got the chance.

'Since he'd only put tape over my mouth and left my hands free I decided to write a message and drop it out somewhere along the way without him seeing me.

'Of course he wouldn't let me keep my mobile phone but he did let me keep my handbag …after searching it of course.

'The only thing in it I could write on was one of the banknotes in my purse and only thing I had to write with was a lipstick.

'So soon after he drove off from our town house I started writing the note by using Morse code for help … dot-dot-dot then dash-dash-dash then three more dots … something I learned years ago when I was a girl.

'That was simple enough. The real problem was to write something that would give a clue as to where I was being taken.

'But because I had no idea where we were going I couldn't write anything on the note until we actually got there and then of course it might be too late.

'But in the end I was lucky.

'When we arrived at that place where he held me he had to stop to open the gates. And since the house was on the high side of the road the car was pointing upwards and that's when I saw those numbers.'

'I wrote them under the SOS and dropped the note out the window while he was opening the gates. Luckily for me he seemed to have a lot of trouble with the gates which gave me plenty of time to copy the numbers.

'And the open window was on the passenger's side of the car so there was no chance he'd see the $10 note as he came back to the car.

'I didn't have much doubt that someone would find it … after all, who leaves a ten dollar note just lying around on the ground.

'But I was afraid that no one would bother to try to make any sense out of what I'd written on it.'

Hodgkiss smiled. 'Luckily for you it fell into the right hands, eventually.'

Just then they heard the sound of Donald's unmarked police car pull up in the drive way. Moments later Donald appeared around the side of the house.

Hodgkiss rose from his bench. 'Well, Donald. I assume you got my message about the number plate of the vehicle that wretched Anstey fellow was driving.'

Donald nodded. 'Yeah. Sure did. We picked him up as he was driving out of his town house.'

'Excellent. And may I assume that he is safely under lock and key, where he belongs?' he demanded.

Donald shook his head. 'He called his lawyer and he's out on bail.' He slid onto the bench beside Esme.

'I suppose I should be angry at you and Pat for running off and doing your own thing once again without telling me first. You realise your little adventure could have ended very nastily. You should have rung me and I'd have come along and dealt with Anstey.'

'Really?' Hodgkiss sneered. 'If I'd rung and asked for your assistance you would have laughed in my face … as you usually do.'

'That's enough of that, Dad,' Esme cautioned. 'Everything's turned out for the best so there's no need for you to start making things unpleasant.'

'Yes, but things only turned out for the best, as you put it, because Pat and I made things happen. If we'd left it to Donald, Amelia here would have still been trussed up like a chicken in strange house. Or worse. We have no idea what he intended to do with her. Obviously he couldn't just let her go after what he'd done.'

Donald shook his head angrily. 'You seem to have conveniently forgotten that I distinctly told you and Pat that if you could make sense of those numbers I'd see what I could do to help. But what did you do? Did you contact me? No. The two of you decided to run off on a little frolic of your own and it could have finished very badly for all three of you.'

'We acted on our own only because we had no confidence whatever that you would see fit to cooperate,' Hodgkiss said loftily.

'That's enough you two,' said Esme. 'Now, what I'd like to know is how Pat worked out where Mr Anstey had taken Amelia.'

'Yeah, that's something I'd like to know too,' said Donald. 'I suppose it was those numbers on the note that were the clue?'

'Of course it was the numbers,' Hodgkiss snapped. 'What did you think it was? Guesswork or perhaps some supernatural power.'

'Be quiet, Dad, and let Pat tell us,' said Esme.

Pat began. 'I had a feeling that I'd seen numbers like that before; numbers that were too big to be a house number but not big enough for a phone number.

'Then it came to me.

'Do you remember a few years back when some of the Jewish people in St Ives wanted to build an eruv?

'Yes,' said Esme. 'They wanted special wires strung from the power poles to enclose a particular area where they wouldn't have to follow all their odd strict religious rules at the weekend about what they could and couldn't do.'

Pat nodded. 'That's right. And council wouldn't allow them to put up the extra wires so they went to the power company and they agreed to let them run their wires up the sides of the power poles inside plastic conduits so that they made contact with the overhead wires. That's how they got around it. At the time I was interested in what was happening and I remember looking at the poles that had these special conduits attached to them.

'I noticed then that each power pole has a small metal plate nailed to it with a number on it.

'Many of these numbers had five or six figures.

'Of course as soon as I remembered that I went straight back to Boston Street where the note was found and looked at the numbers on the power poles.

'I took only a few minutes to find the pole with the same number as Amelia had written on the ten dollar note. It was about in the middle of the block.

'So I decided the pole with the same number as the note would be outside the house where Amelia was being held.

'To make sure I made enquiries at one of the neighbouring houses.

'I spoke to a woman there and she told me that the owner of the house next door was away. Then after I'd asked a few more questions she mentioned that a strange car had arrived there in the middle of the night on Monday or early Tuesday morning and she'd seen a strange man walking around in the back yard behaving in a rather agitated manner.'

'An excellent outcome,' Hodgkiss announced. 'Now the

only question remaining is what is to be done with the ten dollar note?'

Without waiting for a reply he continued. 'I think we should have it framed and display it at some appropriate location as a perpetual reminder of Pat's ingenuity.'

'Nonsense,' Esme snapped. 'It would cost more than ten dollars to frame the thing.'

Her hand shot out and in a moment the plastic envelope containing the note was resting in her lap.

'It's going towards my housekeeping.'

Hodgkiss knew from the look on his daughter's face that argument would be futile.